AS ABOVE, SO BELOW

KAREN HASTIE

This edition published by Here Be Dragons Limited 2020

8.2

Feb 2025

1

PROLOGUE

Just south of London Wall, in the heart of the City of London stands a Grade II listed building. Wood Street Station is the home of the City of London Police force. Dedicated to policing the square mile that is the financial district of the capital. Its grey Portland stone facade, designed in the style of an Italian Palace stands at the corner of Wood Street and Love Lane.

2

HARLOT

Leadenhall Street, London. Wednesday, November 27. 17:30

Rain sweeps over London in thin sheets of grey, draining the city of light.

He lets the tears of heaven fall onto his face, savouring the cleansing chill of the water as it runs under the collar of his coat.

Sent by God to wash away their sins, he tells himself, his gaze following the tide of rubbish flowing down the gutters until it disappears into the dark sewers below.

Sheltering beneath the stone facade of the old East India House, he watches the approaching storm darken the sky, dimming the last of the winter sun and lowering the temperature. Condensation fogs the windows of the warmly-lit restaurant on the opposite side of the street, obscuring the outside world.

Only a few degrees lower and ice crystals would form, he thought. *Liquid becomes solid. Matter transformed. Such was the ever-changing beauty of nature.*

. . .

Through the main doors, he can see the woman sitting alone at the bar of the restaurant. A large glass of wine stands untouched beside her. Her eyes flicker constantly from the entrance to her phone, she shifts uncomfortably on her stool, like an impatient dog waiting for the return of its master.

She looks younger than he imagined, perhaps in her mid-thirties, her hair tinted with the salts of peroxide and ammonia. *Dressed like a harlot*, her silk blouse unbuttoned to reveal a hint of the expensive lingerie she would have spent hours pondering over while her husband was asleep. Her skirt falls gracefully off her long slender legs and her lipstick is a shade more daring than the one she wears for work.

A desperate attempt to make herself more appealing to her lover.

A police Range Rover passes in front of him along Leadenhall Street, blocking his view. He retreats into the shadows. He is in no particular hurry to begin and it amuses him to watch her look of hopeful expectation at every stranger that wanders in out of the storm; enjoying the knowledge that her lover isn't coming.

Time passes and the bar begins to fill with customers. The opaque windows obscure the faces of the diners, twisting them into strange caricatures.

Their masks slipping to reveal their inner demons.

The rain falls harder now, leeching the colour from the street, turning everything to monochrome. Passing commuters sprout umbrellas like so many rows of dark flowers, momentarily blocking his view of her.

It didn't matter, he knows where she will be going.

Straight to hell.

Taking out his phone, he sends the text message.

3

CRIME SCENE

St Mary Axe, London. Thursday, November, 28. 07:00

DS Philippa Marshall stepped out of the car into the bitter cold. Dawn was breaking and the heavy storm clouds hanging over Canary Wharf were painted with the kind of pink glow that always threatened snow. She blew into her hands, wishing she hadn't left her gloves at home, and pushed them deep into the pockets of her winter coat.

Her breath turned to smoke as she walked up Leadenhall towards the cluster of police vehicles. *Dragon's breath,* they had called it as kids and she still found it surreal to think the swirling vapour had just been inside her lungs.

This was her first serious case since returning to active duty, and the first murder in the city for almost three years. Most of the crimes in the square mile were financial. The City of London Police CID dealt mainly with fraud, robberies and serious assaults. Murders were rare, so this would be treated as a major incident, a 'career-maker' as her boss would call it.

Marshall was on the early shift when the call came in and the first detective on the scene. In a couple of hours the senior team would be crawling over this like maggots on a three-day old corpse.

'Detective Sergeant Philippa Marshall,' she said, showing her warrant card to the half-frozen constable holding a clipboard.

For a second, he looked as if he half-recognised the name, then it passed and he wrote it down into his log.

Yes, I'm the one, she thought, ducking underneath the tape. *The one that lost the Malvek case and my baby.*

Before she reached the entrance to the church, the pathologist appeared at the door. Doctor Gates took a deep breath and stretched his back like a man who had just been released from a night in the cells. Gates was in his sixties, close to retiring, and wore the haunted look of a man who had seen too much.

'Marshall.' He nodded, not bothering to acknowledge her rank. 'Nice of you to join us.'

It must be bad, she said to herself, *to have to call Gates out.*

'They'll be needing a few more hours,' he said, looking over at the forensics team who were unloading black cases from the back of a van. 'It's a mess in there.'

'Do you have a time of death?'

He scratched his beard while staring myopically at his watch, as if having to remind himself of the actual time.

'I would hazard somewhere between midnight and three am. Do you have a cigarette?'

She shook her head. 'No.'

Gates grunted, pulling open his Tyvek disposable suit and searching through his jacket pockets. 'Wife tried to get me to use those damn e-things.' He fished out a crumpled packet of Marlboro Reds. 'Can't stand them, create more smoke than a steam engine.'

Placing a crooked cigarette between his lips, he lit it and inhaled deeply.

'Cleaner found the victim at five-thirty this morning. She's with your DC over yonder.' He pointed towards an ambulance. Matthew Biggs was taking notes from a small, dark-haired woman who was wrapped in a blanket and weeping into her hands.

Biggs looked up and nodded a greeting. He was a young, fresh-faced graduate, two years out of university, but she liked him. He had a kind of irrepressible optimism that reminded her of why she had joined the force in the first place.

Marshall looked past him and along the street. Police vehicles were blocking the road in both directions and two of the SOCO support vans were parked strategically to block the view of the entrance to the church.

She spotted CCTV cameras on each side of the road, all of which had clear lines of sight on the entrance. It was one advantage of being in the heart of the financial district, the square mile that was the City of London — it was possibly the most heavily monitored area in the UK.

'What did she find?'

'Female, late thirties.'

'Cause of death?'

He coughed, it had the hoarse rattle of a man who'd smoked all his life. 'Your guess is as good as mine right now.'

'Can I go in?'

The pathologist threw away the cigarette, and fished a paper suit out of one of the black cases.

'You eaten yet?'

Marshall shook her head, unbuttoning her coat.

'Probably for the best. I hate to see a breakfast go to waste.'

There was an unnatural stillness to churches that Marshall always found creepy. It was a silence that seemed to have many parts: like the lingering pause between a question and an answer mixed with the emptiness of an abandoned house.

Walking along the nave, she could count on her fingers the times she had been in a church. The wedding of her best friend, the christening of her cousin's baby and the funerals of three friends.

She had an aversion to family gatherings, especially in churches. It was verging on a phobia according to her mother, but as far as Marshall was concerned, nothing good ever came of stepping inside God's house.

The staircase to the crypt was a curving set of stone steps, like something from the tower of a castle. They were worn from hundreds of years of use. Following behind Gates, Marshall studied the walls for signs of a struggle. *It would have been difficult to drag a body down here, especially if she was still conscious.*

There was nothing obvious to the naked eye, but she knew Gates and his team had other ways, processes that could "lift a fingerprint from a fly's arse", as he would so eloquently put it.

The crypt was crowded with members of the SOCO team carefully studying every square inch of the stone chamber. At the far end, lit by bright LED lamps, the victim appeared to be kneeling at the altar of a small chapel. A statue of the Blessed Virgin smiling beatifically down at her.

From behind, the woman looked as though she was praying, except there was something strange etched onto the bare soles of her feet. Squatting down to study the marks, Marshall could see that the skin had blistered around the symbols as if they had been burned in using a soldering iron.

"Observe without assumption," her old sergeant used to remind her, back when she used to walk the beat. "The first impressions of a crime scene are the most critical."

The body still had the faint aroma of perfume, an expensive scent, like Chanel or Dior. Marshall was relieved, she had smelled a lot worse over the last fifteen years.

Waving the photographer over. 'Close up on these please,' she said, getting to her feet.

The woman was naked. Her body rigid where rigor mortis had stiffened the muscles. Her pale skin was waxy and purple bruising dappled her buttocks where her heels pressed into them.

Walking around to face her, Marshall had to stifle a cry. The woman's hands had been bound with barbed wire, clasped together in prayer. Dried blood ran down her arms and over her breasts. She had been posed like a nun, or a bride on her wedding day.

A pillow lay beneath her knees, the heads of two long nails protruded from each thigh where she had been pinned in position. Marshall winced at the thought of the pain she would have endured, shivering at the visions of the killer hammering the nails into her legs.

But it was her face that had taken the worst of the

punishment. Her mouth was held open by some kind of metal device strapped around her head, it was wedged between her jaws, forcing her mouth unnaturally wide.

Staring into the dark gaping hole that was her ruined mouth, Marshall could see why.

So that he could cut out her tongue.

4

INVESTIGATION BEGINS

Wood Street Police Station, London. Thursday, November 28. 11:05

The briefing had already started when Marshall walked into the incident room. It was standing room only, everyone wanted to be in on this one. DC Biggs had saved her a seat, greeting her with his usual cocky smile.

'Sorry guv,' she apologised to DCI Donovan dropping into the chair beside Biggs.

'DS Marshall,' Donovan acknowledged, turning back to a large plasma screen displaying a map of the area and images from the crime scene.

Acting Detective Inspector Salazar stood beside him, looking like a disapproving school teacher with her arms folded.

She's not happy with me coming back, Marshall thought, smiling at the pinched-face woman. Although she recognised most of the other people in the room, there were a few new faces. *She's brought in some new blood while I was away, trying to build her own little empire.*

Salazar transferred into the squad after Palmer, the previous inspector, had taken early retirement. The position should have gone to Marshall, but she was signed off for three months after losing the baby. She didn't need a crystal ball to know that Salazar was going to make her life hell, the woman made no secret of her intention to make the role permanent.

'So what do we know?' Donovan asked the room, his gaze landing on DC Biggs. 'Boy Scout?'

Biggs stood and opened his notebook.

'The body was discovered by the cleaner at five-thirty this morning. The curate locked up at six the previous evening. No obvious signs of a break-in. The church doesn't have an active congregation, basically just bible study and prayer groups. It's not open to the general public after six. There's a back entrance to the kitchen, which has a dodgy lock, wouldn't have taken much force to get in.'

Salazar took over. 'CCTV?'

'They had a camera installed three years ago after a burglary, but the hard drive packed up two months back and they haven't got the budget to replace it.'

The inspector ground her teeth. She had a hard, angular face made more severe by the tightly pulled pony-tail. Marshall had heard through various sources that she was a career copper more interested in statistics than solving cases. There was a rumour she was shagging someone in internal affairs, the irony of which seemed to be lost on most of the others, but it still made Marshall smile.

'Check with control about the cameras covering Leadenhall and St Mary Axe. She must have been taken there,' Salazar said, tapping on the map.

Biggs nodded and sat down.

The DI swiped through a slideshow of grizzly photographs. 'I think we can all agree this wasn't a domestic. Looks more like a ritual killing wouldn't you say, DS Marshall?'

Marshall didn't stand. She hated being the centre of attention and she didn't like making assumptions — *stick to the facts*.

'Preliminary time of death was somewhere between midnight and three am. Still waiting for pathology to confirm the cause.'

'Apart from the fact he ripped out her tongue!' One of the new officers chipped in, there was a ripple of laughter.

Marshall ignored them, trying hard not to think about the sight of the inside of the victim's mouth.

'The body was posed as if in prayer. Hands bound with barbed wire and nailed in a kneeling position.'

'Sick fuck,' DS Devlin said under his breath. Devlin was ex-army and had spent most of his career in the firearms division. He was a good-looking guy with a chin chiselled out of an action movie and an arrogant attitude to match. He spoke his mind, which Marshall counted as one of his only redeeming features.

Salazar nodded in agreement. 'Let's assume she worked nearby. Marshall, see if you can get a half decent photo from the pathologist. Biggs get down to CCTV. The rest of you get up to speed with the forensics. Baxter you're on missing persons.'

. . .

As they went back to their desks, Donovan caught Marshall's eye and beckoned her to come in to his office.

'Close the door,' he said sternly, sitting down behind his desk.

She did as instructed.

He pulled a folder from one of his drawers. 'I've received the IOPC report on the Malvek case, I thought you might like to read it.'

Marshall shrugged. 'Not especially. I fucked up. What else is there to say?'

Donovan ignored her attitude. After working together for five years, there was no pretension between them, no bullshit.

He opened the document and read from the last page. 'In our opinion, DS Marshall's lapse in judgement did not contribute to the failure of the prosecution.'

'I didn't follow procedure.'

'You were doing your job, the guy was a fucking animal.'

The Malvek case was a domestic that got out of hand. A couple were arrested after fighting in the street following a night of heavy drinking. During the interviews it became obvious that the man was abusing the woman. There were yellowing bruises on her arms and when the doctor examined her, he found evidence of old fractures.

But she wouldn't admit that it was him. The bruise on her lip and the darkening black eye were apparently her own fault.

Whether it was the pregnancy hormones or the broken look in the woman's eyes, Marshall couldn't let it go. When it came time to interview the man, she knew it was up to her to expose him as the abusive bastard that he really was.

Bartosz Malvek was a dark-eyed man with long black hair. He explained in a strong, East European accent, that he was a businessman working for a Polish bank, and that they had simply had a little too much to drink and none of this was any of their business.

At the time they only had him for breach of the peace, or a DnD, but Marshall knew that if they let him off with a caution, his wife would be the one who got punished.

Later, his defence team had insisted that Marshall deliberately provoked him, that her line of questioning had led to him losing his temper.

He punched her so hard in the gut that she miscarried a week later. CPS decided not to pursue the case.

Marshall could have pressed charges, but she didn't. She still wasn't sure why she had pushed him that far. Mrs Malvek checked herself into a women's refuge the day after her husband was released. She had three broken ribs and a fractured cheekbone, but she had kept the card that Marshall gave her during the interview, and that was enough of a victory.

Donovan put the report down. 'Are you sure you're ready for this case?'

She glared at him. 'Do you think I'm not?'

He leaned forward, placing his elbows on the desk. 'No, I know you too well. But off the record, there are some within the team that have their doubts.'

Salazar, she thought.

'Just do everything by the book. Don't give anyone an excuse to question your methods.'

5

CCTV

Thursday, November, 28. 12:00

Biggs stood behind the CCTV operator, staring at a bank of large screens covering the wall in front of them.

'That's Leadenhall,' said the officer, pointing at a group of four monitors showing different views of the same rain-soaked street. The pavements were lined with umbrella wielding commuters on their way home.

'Fucking brollies,' the operator grumbled. 'Totally screws up the face recognition.' He pointed to the small white squares floating over the heads of those passing under the camera. The sea of black canvas was making it impossible to pick up anyone clearly.

The timecode on the screen read 18:20:22 and continued to count in double time as the man scrubbed through the next two hours.

Biggs looked around the control room. A dozen men and women sat behind their desks staring blankly into the glow of their screens. He couldn't imagine a more mundane job, spending day after day watching the world pass by in a darkened room. It was why he had chosen the police instead of joining the family business. He wanted to escape the monotony of the daily grind; the commute and the nine to five. He was fast-tracked straight out of university, two years later he made it into CID and he was loving every minute of it.

As the time moved forward, the stream of commuters dwindled to nothing and the empty streets became the hunting ground of the homeless. They appeared like ghosts, shuffling out of alleys and rummaging through bins. According to the timecode, it was past eleven before the bars and pubs were beginning to empty.

Biggs sighed, rubbing his eyes. 'Switch to St Mary's and let's start from five.'

The old church stood stoically at the corner of Leadenhall and St Mary Axe. A fifteenth-century relic surrounded by modern architectural monoliths including the Gherkin and the Lloyd's building.

They watched as the streets quickly crowded with raincoats and umbrellas, everyone hunched against the weather, all making their way back to Liverpool Street station.

'They reckon it's going to rain for a solid month,' the operator said, trying to fill the awkward silence. Biggs was standing so close that he could smell the man's cheap deodorant. It was the kind that teenage boys bought hoping to get laid. This guy was grossly overweight and sweat patches were appearing across the back of his shirt.

I'm making him nervous.

'Stop!' Biggs snapped. 'Can you zoom in on her?' he asked, pointing towards a woman running across the road. There was something about the way she moved, she seemed distracted, completely oblivious to the rain.

The operator brought the feed up on his main monitor and selected an area of the screen with a pudgy finger. They watched the image expand, softening as the software enhanced the image, blurring her face as it enlarged.

'She's not heading home,' Biggs murmured to himself. 'Can you bring up the same timeframe from Leadenhall?'

The man tapped a sequence of keys and the screen split to show the feeds from the two streets sitting side by side. The timecode read 17:53.

'Now go back slowly.'

The footage reversed and they followed her light coloured coat as she rushed against the flow of commuters, until they traced her back to the bar.

'Rebellion,' noted Biggs.

6

POST MORTEM

Westminster Mortuary, London. Thursday, November 28. 12:10

The victim's body was laid out on a steel table. The grey, pallid skin of her chest was folded back exposing a gaping cavity. Some of her internal organs were already sitting in steel dishes on the trolley beside the pathologist.

Gates looked like a mad scientist, with his frizzy grey hair and smears of blood down the front of his gown where he had wiped his hands.

He's a legend, she reminded herself, *he worked on the Nilsen case back in the eighties.*

'DS Marshall, I'm afraid the post mortem report won't be ready for another day or so,' the pathologist said, picking up a pair of steel forceps. 'But you're just in time to see the most interesting part,' he added, with a little too much enthusiasm.

Marshall walked over to the body. Her nose wrinkling at

the overpowering smell of the chemicals which were only just masking the stench of decaying meat.

Glorified butchers, her sergeant used to call them. He was never a big believer in the science behind forensic pathology, preferring good old-fashioned deduction. Fingerprints were only just acceptable and the mention of DNA used to make him break out in a cold sweat.

'I need a decent shot of her face,' she said, looking down at the woman. She was relieved to see the contraption had been removed from her mouth.

The pathologist grunted, plunging the forceps into the chest cavity and moving them up underneath her lungs.

'They should be on the system in the next hour or so. No need for you to come all the way down here for that.'

He was right of course, Salazar had sent her on a pointless errand to demonstrate her superiority. Marshall didn't mind. She was happy to get the chance to examine the wounds for herself, away from the circus of the crime scene. Preferring to hear what Gates had to say rather than wait to read it in a report. It was harder to ask the man to clarify something days later.

'Any idea what killed her?'

He lifted out each lung carefully, placing them on a tray. Then held the corpse's chin while he made a deep incision into her windpipe.

'If I'm not mistaken,' he said, balancing his glasses on the end of his nose and reaching inside her throat with the forceps. 'The cause of death will be asphyxiation.'

He pulled out a small black parcel.

'Is that a —'

'Nokia 3310.'

Marshall's voice cracked a little, she could feel her throat closing up. 'She choked on a phone?'

'After he removed her tongue.' Gates pressed the power button and the screen lit up. 'Incredibly resilient model. Great battery life,' he added, wiping the blood from the display with his thumb.

'Shouldn't you be checking for prints?' she wondered aloud.

He shook his head. 'There were traces of latex residue on her face. The killer was wearing gloves. If there were any latents on this they would have been destroyed by the pharyngeal reflex let alone the blood and saliva.'

He showed her the display, there was a simple text message: 'Running late. Meet you at The Sterling in 5.'

Marshall pulled on a pair of latex gloves and took the phone from him.

'Ten quid says that's her pimp,' Gates said, returning his attention to the chest cavity.

'Cheap phone,' Marshall agreed, scrolling through the previous messages. They were all from the same number. 'Pay-as-you-go.'

Gates took out her stomach and dropped it into a dish. 'Hookers use them all the time. Want to know what she had for her last meal?'

Marshall shook her head and sealed the phone up in an evidence bag. 'Mind if I take it with me?'

'Fine by me. Just sign the form on your way out.'

She walked around the corpse. The woman was in good shape, her legs were shaved, as was her bikini line. Gates had washed her hands, her nails were polished and there was a faint white band where a wedding ring should have been. Her arms were clear of marks except for the puncture wounds from the barbed wire.

'So why go to all this trouble?' Marshall muttered to herself.

'Torture game that went wrong?' Gates replied, lifting out her liver. 'Some kind of fetish thing that went too far. The barbed wire bindings were done while she was still alive. After he cut her tongue out, she would have passed out from blood loss and shock. Then he forced the phone into her throat and she asphyxiated.'

'Was there any sign of sexual trauma?'

Gates shook his head. 'Not that I can find. Whoever did this was more interested in punishing her.'

Marshall stopped at the woman's feet. 'And these marks?'

He put down the liver and came to the end of the table. 'Now that is possibly the next most interesting part of the puzzle. They look like brands, cattle rancher style, but it's actually been made with acid,' he said, sniffing one of her feet.

The man had spent so long around corpses that he had lost all inhibitions around the dead. They were no longer people to him, just so many hundreds of pounds of meat.

She twisted her head to get a better view. 'Do you know what they mean?'

'Looks Masonic to me. Not that I'm into that kind of thing.' He smirked. 'Haven't had time to look them up, need to leave something for your lot to do.'

7

REBELLION

Rebellion, Leadenhall Street, London. Thursday, November 28. 13:05

DC Biggs arrived just after one o'clock to find the bar packed with well-dressed city types making the most of their lunch hour. It was one of those converted banks, a large open space with four floors and private party rooms. A long marble-topped bar ran down one side where he guessed the counters used to be and the wall behind it was lined with every kind of spirit. Biggs had skipped breakfast and his stomach groaned at the smell of the over-priced burgers.

He flashed his ID to a cute-looking waitress and was quickly shown to the manager's office.

The furniture was in keeping with an old bank, there were shelves and cabinets of dark wood, and his desk had a green leather inlay like something from the 1920s.

The manager was a lean, thin man in his early thirties. His smile was a well-practised one, but his eyes were hard and impassive, not giving anything away, this was a man who was used to being questioned by the police.

There was a hint of a Russian accent when he spoke.

'How can I help you detective?'

'I need to look at your CCTV from last night.'

The manager seemed to relax. Whatever he was hiding, it wasn't to do with last night. Biggs had an innate ability to tell when someone was lying, or holding something back. This guy was guilty of something, it just wasn't his problem right now.

The man waved to a door at the back. 'No problem. The CCTV is in the vault.'

'DVR?' Biggs asked, noting that the man hadn't asked what for.

'Of course, state-of-the-art SSD raid drives. Forty-eight hours easy.'

They walked down the back stairs and into yet another bar. This one was closed. The staff were polishing glasses and restocking the shelves.

'Big party last night,' explained the manager, walking between the tables. Biggs saw the way the female staff avoided eye contact with him. They all had sharp, Slavic cheek bones and dark black hair. *There was going to be little point in interviewing the staff*, he thought, *they would be too scared of losing their jobs or worse.*

The CCTV was in a small room next to the Champagne bar. It had once been the strong room, the vault of the Midland Bank, the manager explained.

Four monitors, one for each floor, were bolted to the wall and each screen was split into six feeds. The manager tapped on the keyboard and brought up the files from the previous night on one of the screens.

'What time?'

'Around six. I'm looking for a woman, mid-thirties.'

The manager gave Biggs a look as if to say: 'I can arrange that,' then changed his mind and turned his attention to finding the appropriate video.

'We have six cameras on each floor. They rotate on twenty-second intervals,' he explained, scrubbing through the movie.

They watched in double-time as the bar filled with customers. Groups of friends gathered at the bar and then moved out onto the various tables. A woman sat alone on the ground floor. In the swirl of people she stood out like a rock in the middle of a river. Not touching her drink, she kept her eyes fixed on the entrance, obviously waiting for someone, intermittently checking her phone for messages.

'That's her,' said Biggs, producing a USB stick. 'Copy it onto this.'

Standing outside, Biggs looked towards the church. It was less than a five minute walk. The day was dry and clear, but the streets were busy with the lunchtime rush. He started along Leadenhall, wondering where the victim was going in such a hurry. Keeping his eyes open for possible points where the killer could have been watching her.

His phone started vibrating.

'Biggs,' DS Marshall's voice said. 'Where are you?'

'Just found her last location. A bar on Leadenhall Street.'

'Good, meet me back at the station. Post mortem just gave us our first solid lead on the victim.'

Biggs changed direction and started back towards Bank. His stomach growled again, but lunch would have to wait.

8

PHONE NUMBERS

Wood Street Police Station, London. Thursday, November 28. 15:00

When Marshall returned to the incident room it was virtually empty. Most of the other teams were out chasing up leads. DCI Donovan was on the phone in his office having a tense conversation. By the look on his face it had to be the superintendent and it wasn't going well. The clock was ticking, they were eight hours in and they had yet to identify the victim. She knew there would be internal discussions going on upstairs about budgets, about handing the case over to the superior resources of the Met, and Donovan was doing his best to convince his boss that was a bad idea.

DI Salazar held up the bag with the mobile phone. It slid around inside the plastic like an organ transplant.

'He choked her with it?' she said in a tone that was part

question and part disbelief, her finely-plucked eyebrows arching slightly.

'It's still working,' Marshall said. 'Gates switched it on and showed me the last text.'

Salazar handed it back to her. 'Get it down to tech-ops and have them pull all the data and check the SIM. I want to know who was sending her messages.'

'I don't think it'll help. This isn't the kind of phone you buy for keeps. It's only ever received messages from one number.'

The DI glared at her. 'You have a better idea?'

'I think we should just try calling it.'

Before Salazar could respond. DC Biggs walked in carrying a take-out, he held it up and shook it.

Marshall shook her head slightly. He took the hint and made straight for his desk.

DCI Donovan opened his door. 'You two. In here now.'

'The Super says the Met are sniffing around. He's bought us another twelve hours to come up with something. I don't need to stress how badly this will look on us if we can't even give the poor woman a name.'

Salazar held up the evidence bag. 'We have her phone and it's still working. I was about to try calling the last number on it.'

Donovan's hang-dog expression brightened for a brief second. 'Good! Now that's the kind of left-field thinking that gets things done,' he said it as if it was some important career lesson for Marshall.

She could feel her fingernails digging into her palms, but she kept quiet. No one liked a smart-arse. Especially one that had been passed over for a chance at Inspector.

Marshall bit her tongue while watching Salazar put on the latex glove and take the phone out of the bag. It was slippery and covered in blood and mucus. Salazar hated the sight of blood, how she ever made it as far as she did was a mystery.

Because she knew how to play the game, Marshall had to remind herself.

The screen lit up and Salazar tentatively scrolled through the menu options until she found the contacts.

There was only one number. It simply read 'Jacob', there was no second name.

Unable to bring it close to her ear, she dialled the number and put it on speaker.

It rang six or seven times before a man's voice answered.

'Where the hell have you been? I waited for hours.'

'Jacob, this is Detective Inspector Salazar.'

There was a pause, seconds passed as the man's mind processed the reasons why a police inspector would be calling him.

'Melanie?' he replied, his voice heightened by stress.

'Sir,' the DI continued calmly, 'we need to know who this phone belongs to. You were the last person to contact her.'

Marshall winced internally at Salazar's statement. *She might as well have said 'last person to speak to her before she died...'*

A constant tone cut in as Jacob dropped the call.

Marshall knew that in less than a minute he would have pulled the SIM and dumped the phone.

Donovan looked sternly at Salazar, the anger flushing his cheeks.

'Get it down to HTCU now,' he said through clenched teeth. 'See if they can get a trace on the GPS.'

Salazar left for the High Tech Crime Unit without another word.

Biggs was reviewing the CCTV from the bar on his laptop when Marshall followed Salazar out of the DCI's office. He could see from their expressions that something had gone wrong, but decided it was better not to ask.

'Sarge,' he nodded to the bag. 'Thought you'd need a boost.'

Marshall opened the bag and pulled out the chocolate shake. 'Not great for my diet, Biggs.'

He laughed. 'What diet?'

She sat down next to him. 'Fuck off. Wait until your metabolism slows down and just staring at a burger puts on two pounds.'

'But you're a veggie, plants don't make you fat.'

'Tell that to my arse.' She took a long slow draw on the milkshake. 'Now, show me what you've got.'

He turned his laptop towards her and replayed the last few minutes of the video before she left the bar.

'Hello Melanie,' Marshall whispered to the screen as they watched her sitting at the bar. 'Who is Jacob?'

'Jacob?' Biggs asked, before taking a bite of his burger.

'We found a phone,' she said, sparing him the details while he was eating. 'A burner. There was only one number on it.'

'Lover?'

'Gates thinks it was her pimp.' She peered at the screen. 'Does she look like a hooker to you?'

'A high-end one maybe. The manager at the bar was up to something dodgy. Probably renting out the staff.'

'She looks too tense, look at her body language.'

'I thought it was a bit odd that she didn't use a smart phone,' he said, freezing the video as Melanie checked the small mobile for the third time.

'She was meeting someone. Did any of the bar staff know her?'

Biggs shook his head. 'Busy place. The manager said he'd seen her a couple of times. Hardly touches her drink and then leaves as soon as she gets a text.'

'Does she always pay in cash?'

Biggs's eyes widened as he realised what she was asking. 'Bollocks.'

She grabbed his fries and began to eat them. 'Back you go.'

9

GPS

Wood Street Police Station, London. Thursday, November 28. 16:00

Thirty minutes later Marshall received a curt email from Salazar making some lame excuse about being called into a meeting with the top brass and ordering her to chase up the phone evidence. After the mess that the DI had made of the call it wasn't surprising. Her arse was made of Teflon, nothing ever stuck to it, but Marshall could see that Donovan was still fuming as Salazar left and was secretly glad about it.

Data extraction from the SIM card could take hours, but Salazar had put it through as a fast track job, so it should have been expedited by the cybercrime team.

Marshall walked down three flights to the High Tech Crime Unit. They were part of the digital forensics division: a team of specialists who could extract data from virtually any device or computer, given enough time. Their lead investigator was called Frazer Caldwell, he was a classic geek who shunned the formal suit and tie of the other departments, preferring to wear a hoodie, converse trainers and t-shirts with superhero logos. Rumour was that Frazer had a fortune in bitcoin stashed away and that he saw himself as a modern-day Bruce Wayne; fighting crime without a cape. She was pretty sure he'd started that himself.

Marshall watched Frazer's screen fill up with the text history from the phone. There were hundreds of messages, their entire love story written out in 160 character moments. It was kind of romantic and sad. Melanie was clearly smitten with this Jacob. Who was obviously not her pimp. *Should have taken Gates's bet.*

'Nokia 3000 series, most successful mobile phone ever made,' he said, nodding at the disassembled unit on his desk. 'Legendary battery life.'

'So I hear.'

Marshall had never quite understood what it was about blokes and tech. They seemed to get a kick out of knowing the most inane details about stuff. To her they were simply tools, a useful accessory, but guys seem to see them as symbols of status.

'Can you identify the owner?'

He shook his head. 'Pay-as-you-go SIM, bought for cash over a year ago. The IMEI on the handset puts it at around 2017. There's no useful personal detail in the texts, only dates and times. All of which correlate with the GPS tracking.' He opened a new window and plotted the points across a map of the City of London. A spider web of dots showing the journey the phone had taken over the last six months all radiating out from one central location. 'Looks like she always kept it switched off until she leaves work.' He pointed to a building on Leadenhall Street. 'Based on the pattern, I would say she worked in or within 30 metres of the Lloyd's building.'

'Can you trace the other number?' Marshall asked.

'Already done,' Frazer said proudly, typing a string of code into another terminal window. A cloud of small dots appeared, clustered over the Lloyd's building. 'He was active up until an hour ago. I would guess he's either a colleague or was at her place of work asking about her.'

Marshall smiled and took out her phone. 'Good work,' she said, dialling Biggs's number. 'Biggs, are you at the bar? Okay, stay there I'm coming down.'

10

LLOYD'S

Leadenhall Street, London. Thursday, November 28. 17:00

The Lloyd's building towered over Leadenhall Street, its metal ducts and exposed pipework making it look more like an oil rig than an office building.

Marshall was only two when it was completed in 1986, but she could still picture her father raving about its originality over dinner. He was a lecturer in architecture and would take her to see it whenever they made the trip up to London.

In those days, the city was a place of wonder and awe to her overactive imagination. She always loved their adventures. Her father knew so much about the history of the grand buildings. He became her personal tour guide, the best one she could ever wish for. Although, much to his dismay, she preferred the Palladian architecture of Wren and Webb or the museums and galleries built during the reign of Victoria and Albert. There was something majestic and fairytale about them. No trip was complete until they had visited Buckingham Palace, which used to drive her poor father insane.

The moment they surfaced out of the tube station at Bank, she would begin to plead with him to take her to see the "Fairy Castles", in the petulant way that only a seven-year-old could. He would always try to persuade her that the Lloyd's building was more interesting, explaining how it was 'such a radical departure from the norm', standing there holding her small hand while he stared up at the steel edifice.

Marshall never understood what he saw in it. Not even now.

She came to London seventeen years ago, leaving her parents behind in Bath. All those years on the force had given her a very different view of the city.

Biggs was standing at the entrance to the building when she arrived. He looked very pleased with himself, like a kid who got a bike for Christmas. Marshall wondered if there were times when he still was asked for ID in the pub.

'Melanie Gladwell,' he said, holding up a credit card receipt in an evidence bag. 'Worldpay was down last night so they had to resort to old-fashioned signed dockets.'

The reception area of Lloyd's was a vast steel and concrete atrium. Two heavy-set security guards hovered near the entry gates, both with necks as thick as their heads. They watched Marshall and Biggs approach the front desk with practised disinterest.

'Good afternoon.' The receptionist gave them her best corporate smile. 'How can I—'

They held their warrant cards up in unison, like synchronised swimmers, changing the expression of the woman in mid-sentence.

'We need to speak to Melanie Gladwell,' Marshall asked before the woman had time to react.

Her face adopted the classic 'rabbit-in-headlights' expression, as her brain tried to think of what to do next.

Biggs stepped in, switching on the charm, reading the woman's name tag. 'Heather, it's important we speak to her. Do you have her direct number?'

Her eyes narrowed slightly as her brain finally began to process the choices. She looked down at her computer. 'I'm not supposed to divulge information regarding employees, it's company policy —'

'We understand,' Biggs spoke in a calm, mid-tone. 'Is it possible we could speak to her boss?'

In the six months that Marshall had worked with Biggs, she had quickly realised he had an innate ability to manipulate people. It was a rare talent, one that she had never been able to master.

The woman looked up from her console. 'She's in risk on the third floor, but she hasn't shown up today. Her manager is Jacob Ballantyne.'

So she was shagging her boss, Marshall thought trying to keep her expression indifferent.

11

JACOB

Lloyd's Building, London. Thursday, November 28. 17:15

Jacob Ballantyne had a corner office on the third floor. It was large, with tall windows that looked directly out over the city. He was a good-looking man in his late thirties. His blonde hair was cropped short, accentuating his cheekbones and framing a pair of bright blue eyes. There were pictures of his wife and children on the desk and framed drawings that were obviously made by his kids hanging on the walls.

He was staring out of the window as they entered.

Six-foot-four, fourteen stone, Marshall estimated. *He would have no trouble lifting a nine-stone corpse.*

'Mr Ballantyne,' she began after his PA closed the door. 'I'm Detective Sergeant Marshall and this is Detective Constable Biggs.'

Ballantyne casually glanced at the warrant cards.

'How can I help you officer?' he said, calmly unbuttoning his Saville Row jacket and sitting back down behind his desk.

Biggs took out his notebook, it wasn't necessary but it made it look more official. 'Can you tell us where you were yesterday evening?'

Marshall caught the subtle movement of his eyes, flicking up to the right, a sure sign he was about to lie.

'I was supposed to meet with a client at the Magpie in Bishopsgate, but they never showed.'

'Which client?' Marshall asked, trying to catch him off-guard.

'Dave Keach from JC Decaux,' he replied without hesitation, as if he had rehearsed it. 'I waited over an hour, but he never showed.'

'Was anyone else there who could corroborate your story?'

He shook his head. 'My guys drink down at Cornhill. What does it matter? I'm sure the bar had CCTV — I spent most of the time on WhatsApp talking to my kids.'

'How well do you know Melanie Gladwell?' Biggs asked.

Ballantyne's lip twitched and his hands clenched slightly. Marshall studied his features, wondering if he was going to continue to lie.

'She works in FR. Financial Risk. I have over two hundred people on my team. Officially I'm her boss, but I probably see her less than once a month.'

Biggs flipped through the pages of his notebook. 'Do you own a mobile phone with a number ending 0989?'

Ballantyne shook his head. 'No, my phone ends 6618,' he said, taking an iPhone out of his suit pocket and placing it on the desk. 'You want me to unlock it?'

'That won't be necessary. When was the last time you saw Melanie?' Marshall continued.

He shrugged and picked up his phone, opening the

calendar app. 'Last week. Tuesday I think,' he said turning the screen towards them. 'FR meeting. 3pm.'

'Do you have her home number? We need to contact her,' Biggs said, making a note of the date.

Ballantyne sneered. 'Why would I have that? You'll need to talk to HR.'

Marshall walked over to the window, so that he had to turn away from Biggs to look at her. 'And she hasn't shown up for work today?'

'No.'

He was beginning to sweat, Marshall noticed small beads of perspiration on his top lip. His fingers were make small fidgeting movements.

'Does that happen often, her not showing up for work?'

'She sometimes works from home, her husband is very ill.'

'Have you heard from her?'

He looked down at his phone. 'No.'

He hasn't asked why we're here. Marshall said to herself.

'I have a meeting in ten minutes, is there anything else?'

'I think we should continue this down at the station,' Biggs suggested.

Marshall agreed.

12

INTERVIEW

Wood Street Police Station, London. Thursday, November 28. 19:00

There was always a point in an interview when Marshall could sense the change. The subject would only be able to hold onto the lie for so long. Either their conscience would get the better of them or they would slip up. Truth was singular and unchanging, easy to recall no matter how many times it was told. Lies were different, they require far more layers of abstraction. Professional criminals were very good at it. Like athletes, they practised deception, training their brain like a muscle until it became second nature. Splitting their minds into two parts, holding dual realities in perfect balance and stepping lightly between each one.

Ballantyne was not a professional, far from it. Instead he was a stoic, saying no more than he needed to, which was nearly as successful, but had one fatal flaw.

What he didn't say told them as much as what he did.

They had explained to him that he was simply helping them with their enquiries and that it would be wise to cooperate, which he duly did. Except when it came to the subject of Melanie.

'How long have you known Melanie Gladwell?' Marshall asked for the second time, after Biggs restarted the tape.

He shrugged. 'About five years.'

'What was she like?' Biggs said.

He's using the past tense. Marshall noted.

The question seemed to throw Ballantyne. It wasn't what he was expecting. *There was that pause again*, she thought, *as his mind tried to find the right thing to say.*

'Good at her job. Kind of quiet, sensible — happy.'

Marshall pictured the words carved onto her gravestone. Not the kind of memorial anyone would choose for themselves. 'Be who you need to be,' her father used to tell her, 'but never be boring.'

Biggs brought out the Nokia wrapped in a clean evidence bag.

'Have you seen this phone before?'

Ballantyne shook his head, but Marshall noticed he was barely able to look at the Nokia.

'So you don't own a similar one?'

'No.'

Marshall leaned forward and took the bag from Biggs. 'It's interesting, there is only one number on it. Hundreds of texts, all seeming to be from someone by the name of Jacob.'

His cheeks flushed a little.

'Were you having an affair?'

Marshall hadn't wanted to be this direct. When they had discussed tactics before the interview she had disagreed with Salazar. It would take a stone-cold psycho to be able to kill a lover and then go back to work the next day as if nothing happened. Marshall knew his type. He was lying to protect his family, his position in the company, but the DI insisted. Salazar wanted the case closed before the press got their hands on it and a dissatisfied lover was a gift in her eyes.

Salazar would be watching on the video in the next room. Marshall should have known better, but she wanted to get to the truth and that meant gaining his trust.

'We know you were seeing her,' she said calmly. 'I don't care what you two got up to. I'm not here to judge you or ruin your life. You're not under caution, so none of this is admissible in court. You're just helping us right now, but if you continue to lie you're going to end up as a suspect.'

He sighed. 'What's happened to her?'

Finally the right question. Marshall took a long, slow breath. There were numerous ways to phrase the next sentence, approaches that she had used many times with the next of kin. There was never a good way to inform someone about the death of a loved one, but she found that generally the factual approach worked best.

'Melanie was found murdered early this morning. She was last seen leaving a bar called Rebellion on Leadenhall Street, after receiving a text on this phone. We believe it was from you.'

He looked stunned. His eyes locked on the evidence bag while he slowly processed the information.

There it is. Marshall watched the poker face crumble away as his expression softened and his whole body seemed to deflate.

'She texted me to meet at the Magpie. We don't go to Rebellion, it's too close to the office.'

'And you stayed there?'

He nodded. 'For nearly two hours. I tried to call her but her phone was off.'

'Does anyone else know about your affair?'

Ballantyne shrugged. 'Some of our co-workers might have guessed. We've been pretty careful. Like I said, I don't fraternise with her at work.'

Marshall looked towards the video camera, wondering how angry Salazar was right now.

'How did you meet?'

He told them the whole story. How she had come back from an extended sick-leave five years ago. Her husband had been diagnosed with a motor neurone disorder and was in need of constant care. Ballantyne had problems of his own at home and somehow they had got talking at a Christmas party and from then on it was an all too familiar story.

Marshall could tell it was the truth, his voice cracked when he talked about the times they were together, how they planned to leave their partners when the time was right — when Melanie's husband died.

Two hours later the CCTV from the Magpie verified his alibi and he was released.

Marshall was not so fortunate. Salazar pulled her into Donovan's office the moment Ballantyne was gone.

'What the fuck was that?' she barked.

Marshall had to suppress a smile. Swearing really didn't suit Salazar, it was like your mum saying the C-word. Some people just shouldn't do it.

'The CCTV proved it wasn't him.'

'But you didn't know that when you were interviewing

him,' Salazar said, raising a finger. 'You ignored a direct order.'

'I went with my gut.'

Salazar turned towards Donovan. 'I want her off my team.'

The DCI winced, he looked like a dad who'd been inadvertently drawn into an argument between two of his daughters.

'That's not your decision to make. She's a good officer and we don't have a lot of options,' he said, raising his hands as if trying to calm the situation down.

'Good officers know how to follow orders.'

Donovan nodded in agreement. 'Resources are tight, we'll be lucky to get another DS in before the weekend. Unless you want to involve the Met.'

Salazar sneered. 'No fucking way.'

Marshall had to look away to stop herself from laughing.

'Then I suggest you find a way to work together. The next twenty-four hours are critical.'

The DI glared at Donovan. 'I want this put on record. You can be responsible for her next fuck up.' She turned and walked out of the room, slamming the door behind her.

Donovan sighed. 'Do you go out of your way to make my life hell?'

'Sir?'

'It took a lot of persuading to get you back on my team. You're a good detective, instinctive, you feel it in your bones. I'd rather have one of you than half of those twats out there.' He nodded to the investigation team who were mostly sat behind their computers. 'Many thought that you should have ended up on traffic after the Malvek case.'

Marshall felt her cheeks blush a little. 'Thank you, sir.'

He loosened his tie and undid the top button of his shirt.

'Procedure requires me to ask you this: Detective Sergeant Marshall do you wish to request a transfer?'

'No, sir.'

He smiled. 'Good, now fuck off and catch the sick bastard before Salazar finds another excuse to have you suspended.'

13

WINE

Calders Wharf, Island Gardens, Docklands. Thursday, November, 28. 21:00

Marshall opened the fridge, relieved to see a near full bottle of Sancerre resting in the wine rack. She pulled out the cold bottle, along with two tinfoil trays of yesterday's takeaway curry and went into the living room.

Putting the meal on the coffee table, Marshall went over to a stack of cardboard boxes and rummaged through them until she found a plate and a spoon then sat down to eat. It had been over a week since she moved in and most of her belongings were still packed or in storage.

When James had transferred to Manchester, she decided it was time for a fresh start. They had been renting a house and Marshall couldn't afford to pay for it on her own. So she found a riverside apartment in Docklands with a great view of Greenwich and a decent security system.

It still felt like she was staying in a hotel. There were none of the homely elements that she had loved about their place in Tooting. That was where they were supposed to be starting a family, or at least it was until she lost the baby.

Marshall was only nine weeks into her pregnancy. The doctor had explained that Malvek's attack might have brought on the miscarriage, but he couldn't say for sure. It was so early that she hadn't really felt that it was there, just a tiny flutter in her stomach and a heightening of her senses — she felt more alive.

Afterwards she just felt empty. James hardly said anything about it, never outwardly blaming her for what happened, but she could see something in his eyes. An unspoken tension grew between them and he began to stay later at work. He was a DI in organised crime and there always seemed to be a reason to take the overtime.

Then he began to drink heavily, even when they went out with friends. So many officers had a problem with booze at some point, but James had always been quite restrained, he wasn't one of the lads. Which was probably why she had fallen for him in the first place.

But when he got drunk, especially on whisky, he became an aggressive, spiteful bastard. It was like Jekyll and Hyde, there was a terrible monster growing inside him.

Their relationship was becoming toxic, he couldn't look her in the eye, let alone sleep in her bed.

So when the offer came to join the National Crime Agency in Manchester he jumped at the chance. They never even discussed it.

The curry was better cold, as was the wine. After pouring another large glass, she opened her laptop and logged in. Images from the crime scene had been loaded onto HOLMES, the police database, and Marshall began swiping through the pictures while shovelling tarka dhal into her mouth.

If it wasn't the lover, she thought, *then it could be the husband.* Ballantyne had told them he dumped the mobile in a bin in Liverpool Street Station and uniform had been dispatched to retrieve it.

Salazar was sending DS Devlin to inform the husband in the morning. It was an odd choice, Devlin wasn't the most subtle of men when it came to emotional situations, but the Inspector was making a point of how unimportant Marshall was going to be on this case. It wouldn't surprise her to find out she was an office manager by tomorrow.

Her phone vibrated, it was a text message from her mother. There were four missed calls from her and at least two voice messages. Marshall took a large slug of the wine and called her number.

'Hi mum, sorry I've been really busy.'

'Hello dear. It's your father...'

It always was these days. Her dad had dementia and her mother was doing her best to cope. It was hard to watch the most important man in your life turning into a complete stranger. There were fewer good days than bad now: often he would be found in a neighbour's house accusing her mother of kidnapping him or mistaking Marshall for his wife while insisting the woman in the kitchen making their dinner was his mother.

The neurologist had warned them it would get progressively worse, and that they would need to think about respite care. But her mother was from that generation that 'made-do' and she wouldn't hear of him being put into a home.

Marshall was her confessor, her only outlet to release all

the pent-up frustration and anger she felt for the slow death of the man she loved.

'He's had some kind of mini-stroke. Half of his face stopped working.'

'Did you call an ambulance?'

'Yes, we've been to the hospital. They called it a T.I.A.'

Transient ischemic attack, Marshall translated. A mini-stroke caused by lack of blood to the brain. Her father had been a fit and healthy man all of his life. A TIA was a sign that something else was going on.

'It was over before the ambulance arrived,' her mother continued. 'The poor man must have thought we were playing a joke on him.'

'You did the right thing, Mum. Did they say what they're going to do next?'

'Yes, we've an appointment at the stroke clinic in three weeks. I thought perhaps you would come?'

Three weeks was literally the week before Christmas, Marshall calculated.

'Yes, of course.'

Merry bloody Christmas, Marshall thought, pouring the rest of the wine into her glass.

She felt the tears stinging at the corners of her eyes and gritted her teeth, pushing down the emotion.

14

THE HUSBAND

Guildford, Surrey. Friday, November 29. 09:30

Donovan had obviously overruled Salazar at some point after Marshall had left, she was still on the case when she woke the next morning.

Ballantyne had told them that Melanie Gladwell lived with her husband in a detached five-bedroom house in a leafy suburban street in Guildford. There was a uniform from the local station standing guard at the front door when Marshall arrived.

Devlin had already delivered the news and left, he was not one to hang around. A family liaison officer opened the door when she knocked.

'DS Marshall,' the woman greeted her, stepping out onto the front porch. 'Before you go in, I just need to make you aware of a few things.'

Marshall nodded and stepped back into the garden.

'Mr Gladwell is very ill. He has Motor Neurone Disease and is in need of twenty-four hour supervision. His carer is with him now. We have informed him that we believe it may be his wife, but he is too sick to make a formal identification. There is a sister apparently, lives in Leeds. We've contacted the local force and they are going to arrange for her to come down.'

'So, can I speak to him?'

The officer nodded. 'Yes, but please be aware that Mr Gladwell has been very distressed since DS Devlin told him.'

I bet he has. Devlin's got as much empathy as a brick wall.

Marshall nodded and walked through the front door.

The ground floor of the house was like a hospital wing. A long room that might have once been the lounge or dining room had been converted into a medical bay. A high-tech bed sat in the centre surrounded by various machines and monitors.

It looks expensive, she thought. *He must have some seriously comprehensive health insurance.*

Melanie's husband was sitting upright in the bed, his face obscured by an oxygen mask. An agency nurse in light blue scrubs was checking his blood pressure as she walked in.

'Mr Gladwell,' she spoke softly, keeping her tone cool and professional.

He nodded, there were still tears in his eyes.

Gladwell was forty-two, five years older than his wife, but his body looked wasted and frail beneath the clean white sheets. Marshall could see there was still a fire in his eyes.

'I'm Detective Sergeant Marshall. I was there when they found your wife. Would it be okay if I asked you a few questions?' she said, taking out her notebook.

He took off the oxygen mask with a hiss. 'Yes.'

'Would you know of any reason why someone would want to harm Melanie?'

He shook his head. 'No, she was a very kind woman. Everybody loved her.'

'Did she mention having any problems at work?'

He blinked back the tears. 'They've been very good to her since the illness. Their healthcare is the only reason I'm still alive.' He nodded to the machines around them.

Marshall picked up one of the framed photos that sat beside his bed. It was from a holiday, somewhere exotic and warm. Obviously taken before he became ill, it showed the two of them smiling. *No kids*, she noted. *But they were happy*.

'How long have you been married?'

His voice grew thin and reedy. 'Fifteen years. We met at Brookes in Oxford. I was training to be a quantity surveyor and she was studying economics. She always joked that we were the most boring couple on campus.' He tried to laugh, but it caught in his throat and he started to cough.

The nurse placed the oxygen mask back on his face, giving Marshall a stern look that said her patience was running low.

Once his breathing settled he nodded for her to continue.

'Did she give up work when you became ill?'

He pulled the mask down. 'No. Five years ago my condition declined rapidly. They gave her extended sick leave so that she could look after me.'

The family liaison walked back into the room with the nurse. She tapped on her watch to indicate that Marshall's time was nearly up. She nodded and put her notebook away.

'Did Melanie say who she was meeting on Wednesday night?'

He shrugged, his bony shoulders hardly moving the baggy gown.

'She mentioned something about a work thing. I got a message from her around five o'clock saying she was going to be staying late. It happens every couple of weeks.'

Marshall picked up another photograph of Melanie and held it up. 'Would you mind if I take a copy of this?'

Gladwell shook his head.

She took a shot of the photo with her phone. There was an unread message from Biggs, but she ignored it and placed the picture back on the shelf.

'Thank you.'

'Did she suffer?' her husband asked, a pained expression on his face. 'The other officer wouldn't tell me.'

'I'm afraid I can't tell you anything more. We won't know until the pathologist has finished the post mortem.'

It was a lie of course, but the truth would probably have killed him.

15

GHB

Wood Street Station, London. Friday, November 29. 14:00

Marshall waited in Donovan's office while Salazar read the report on her laptop. The DI had insisted on taking the spare desk next to Donovan's, enjoying the privilege of being in close proximity to the boss.

As she read, Salazar tapped on her front tooth with one of her manicured fingernails. It was possibly the most annoying noise Marshall had ever had to endure.

'He could have found out about the affair and hired someone,' she said, without looking up from her screen. 'Choking her with the phone was obviously some kind of message.'

Marshall folded her arms and leaned against Donovan's desk. 'Someone was definitely making a statement, but I don't think it was her husband, he's too ill.'

'You're ruling him out because he's sick?' The DI looked up, her eyes were dark and dead. *Like a shark*, thought Marshall.

'There was a lot of expensive medical kit and a full time carer. Why would he kill the person whose health insurance was keeping him alive?'

Salazar looked puzzled, for once she didn't have an answer.

Donovan had been ignoring them, he was trying to type something up on his computer, using one finger on each hand. 'Get the Boy Scout to look into their finances. I don't know of any healthcare plan that funds something to that level. Not even the Police Federation has that kind of package.'

'Don't be so sure, as a senior partner she would have been on at least two-hundred thousand.' Salazar said. 'My cousin is an actuary at Allianz, he started on seventy-thousand a year when he joined.'

Donovan coughed. 'Fuck. I'm in the wrong line of work.'

He was only five years from retirement and it was common knowledge that he had made some serious financial mistakes over the years — not including two failed marriages. The DCI was a good copper, a thief-taker, one who had worked his way up the ladder from uniform, just as Marshall had done. Salazar on the other hand was fast-tracked straight out of university and still had an annoying air of entitlement that usually gets knocked out of you in the first year on the beat.

'So if it's not the lover or the husband where does that leave us?' Salazar asked, raising one eyebrow at Marshall.

'Without a suspect or a motive,' Marshall replied, stating the obvious.

'Has anyone checked the symbols on her feet yet?' Donovan asked, holding up one of the crime scene photos.

'Baxter was going to look into it,' Marshall replied,

looking over at the old office manager sifting through a pile of case notes. 'But he got reassigned.'

'There are other cases,' Salazar said in her defence. 'We can't afford to dedicate five officers to some fetish sex game that went wrong.'

Marshall stood up and stared out at the wall of photographs. 'I don't think it was sexually motivated. We should be asking why he cut out her tongue? Why pose her like that in a church? The killer knew her, she meant something to him. He thought carefully about the ways he was going to punish her.'

'Punish her for what? Bad financial advice,' Salazar said with a condescending sneer.

Marshall ignored her. She could still picture the distorted shape of the victim's mouth. 'For something she said or didn't say.'

Donovan's computer chimed, it was an email from pathology. 'The tox report's back. Looks like she was drugged with GHB.'

Gamma-hydroxybutyric acid or GHB was a common date rape drug. It induced a coma-like state that lasted for up to two hours. Usually slipped into a victim's drink, it left them with no memory of what had happened when they recovered.

At least she didn't suffer.

16

SYMBOLS

Wood Street Station, London. Friday, November 29. 14:30

Biggs was studiously scrolling through a long spreadsheet of financial details when Marshall got back to her desk. The remnants of his lunch was piled up on her side, reminding her that she hadn't eaten anything since breakfast. Fishing out some of the fries, she went around to join him. She caught the pungent aroma of the soggy trainers which were slowly steaming under the radiator, a sign that he had run his usual six miles into the station. Marshall couldn't remember the last time she'd been to the gym and the tightness of her trousers was already reminding her that she needed to get back into shape.

'How was the husband?' he asked, taking out his headphones and pausing the track on his computer.

Taking out her phone, Marshall showed him the picture of Melanie. 'If he knew about the affair he hid it well. I think she was just lonely. He's a very sick man.'

He nodded. 'Motor neurone's a bitch. Most people die within two years, he's doing well to have survived so long.'

'Thanks to her health insurance.'

Biggs shook his head. 'I'm not sure it is. I've been going over their financials for the last five years.' He tapped on the laptop screen, opening a scan of an old bank statement.

'Their current balance is just over half a million.'

As Biggs scrolled down the list of transactions, Marshall could see large sums being paid out to various healthcare companies.

Marshall whistled through her teeth. 'So they're rich?'

'Not until January 2015,' Biggs said, swiping up the screen to a hi-lighted row. 'They received a massive payout that year from the Galena Group.'

'Her husband said that it was part of their healthcare plan.'

Biggs opened up another window. 'Except the Galena Group isn't an insurance firm. I can't find anything about them other than that they're based in the Cayman Islands.'

'Offshore shell company,' Marshall said, folding her arms and sitting on the side of his desk. 'Hardly a reason to kill someone.'

'Maybe it was a kidnap that went wrong?'

'No, they tend to keep the victim in one piece, at least until you need some proof of life. And I'd hardly start with the tongue, would you?'

Biggs shrugged.

'Someone was punishing her.'

'For cheating?'

'If it wasn't him or the lover then someone else knew. Once we find them we might have a chance of solving this.'

. . .

Baxter wandered over in his usual unassuming way. He was in his early sixties, but looked much older. The man had a penchant for cardigans and corduroy trousers, as if he had just stepped out of a seventies knitting pattern. There was always a faint odour of dust about him, mixed with a hint of Deep Heat.

Turning his back to Donovan's office, he pulled out pictures of Melanie's feet from inside his cardigan.

'They're alchemical symbols,' he said quietly, moving the half-moon spectacles to the end of his nose. 'Some have a double meaning.' Baxter pointed at the triangle with the plus sign. 'This is the symbol for sulphur, or the body. And this —' He tapped on the second triangle with a horizontal line through its top half. 'Is the symbol for air.'

'What's so significant about them?' Biggs asked, picking up one of the photographs.

Baxter shrugged. 'No idea.' He stiffened as Salazar came out to speak to Devlin. 'Just don't tell the Wicked Witch of the West that I helped you.'

Marshall nodded and Baxter walked off, humming "Ding dong the witch is dead" to himself.

Biggs looked confused. 'What the fuck is alchemy?'

Picking up one of the photographs, she shuddered, imagining what it must have felt like to have them burned into her skin. 'I have no idea, but let's keep it to ourselves for now.'

Marshall went back to her desk, helping herself to the rest of the fries as she cleared away the debris. Settling into her chair, she opened the tox report on her laptop. Gates's lab had rushed through the analysis on Salazar's orders. All the usual stats were there: blood type, haemoglobin levels, and the rest. She was a very normal human being in all aspects bar one. She was a type I diabetic.

'Biggs,' Marshall said, turning back towards the DC. 'Did we find her bag?'

He shook his head. 'Haven't found her clothes yet, let alone a handbag.'

'Type I diabetics needed to regularly check their sugar levels. She would always be carrying a test kit in case they got too low — prevent her from going into hypoglycaemic shock.'

'Forensics searched the grounds of the church.'

'That was where he took her, not necessarily where he grabbed her.'

17

CAR PARK

St Mary Axe, London. Friday, November 29. 15:30

The church was closed. Police tape fluttered like a kite tail in the cold winds, stirring piles of rubbish around the small garden. A tramp was sleeping on one of the benches, two battered cans of Special Brew rattled around on the floor beneath him.

Marshall stood on the pavement, surveying the street, trying to understand how the killer had moved the body into the church and then undressed her without leaving any physical evidence.

The last footage they had of Melanie was crossing over Leadenhall on her way to The Sterling, a restaurant in the Gherkin. The large glass and steel cone of a building loomed over St Mary Axe like an oversized Christmas decoration — it was less than two minutes away.

She followed the route Melanie would have taken until she reached the Gherkin. Opposite was an entrance to an underground car park. Marshall wandered down to the barriers, looking into the dimly lit space beyond.

'Can I help you with something?' A car park attendant appeared from a small office tucked away out of sight.

Marshall held up her ID. 'Do you mind if I look around?'

The man shrugged. 'Help yourself.'

She ducked under the barrier and he followed.

'Do you have CCTV covering this area.'

He sucked air in through his teeth, nodding towards his cubicle. Four small black and white TVs were stacked on a shelf at the back of his office. 'They're just so I don't have to wander around,' he explained, there's no recording.

'Were you here on Wednesday?'

'I'm here every day,' he said dryly, as though it was some kind of punishment.

'What time does the car park close?'

'It doesn't.'

'And is it manned twenty-four hours?'

He laughed. 'No, I knock-off at six and then its automated. To be fair I don't see the point of me being here really. The whole bloody thing is automatic.'

'Did you notice anything odd when you came in on Thursday morning?'

'You mean other than the police blocking off the road?'

'Yes, I mean no, was there anything down here that was out of place?'

His eyes narrowed, as if he was trying to squeeze something out of his brain.

'Someone left their van here overnight. They still haven't picked it up.'

Marshall looked around the garage. 'Which one?'

He pointed to a service truck in the furthest corner. 'That shit heap.'

'Wait here.'

. . .

Marshall walked over to the old Ford Transit, a thousand thoughts racing through her mind: she should seal off the area and call in the SOCO team immediately, the vehicle could be a goldmine of evidence, APNR tracking through London could give them a trace on where the killer came from. So many possibilities spiralled out from this one find that it was making her head spin. She focused on her breathing, letting her mind clear.

It was parked with the rear against the wall. The red paintwork was dull and mottled, the faint outline of an old logo barely visible. *Royal Mail*

Looking through the driver's window, her hopes began to fade. The interior looked immaculate, none of the usual crap that a builder's cab usually contained. Moving to the back of the van, she found one of the doors slightly ajar and with the rusting hinges complaining, she prised it open with a pen.

Inside the cargo space were clothes, a bag and a pair of shoes. All neatly folded as if they were being displayed in a shop.

OCD, she thought, stepping back and taking a photo with her phone.

There was no signal underground, so she walked back to the barrier.

'Anything?' the attendant asked when she reached his office.

She nodded, putting the phone to her ear.

'Guv, I've found her clothes. Underground car park off St Mary Axe.'

Listening to her, the colour drained from the attendant's

face. She put her hand on his arm, stopping him from walking over to the van.

'Don't go near it. Close this place down,' she whispered to him, while listening to the DCI barking orders at the rest of the team.

'Yes, Biggs is outside. We need to get SOCO down here ASAP.'

'How did he get her in here?' Biggs asked, staring into the back of the van.

'No idea,' Marshall replied.

'He's compulsive.'

'That's what worries me. The cab is immaculate too. I'm worried we're not going to find anything.'

'What about the reg?' Biggs said, staring at the number plate.

She knelt down. 'Screw heads look new. Ten quid says it's stolen.'

'Bollocks,' Biggs swore, staring out towards the exit ramp. 'So how come we didn't find him on the CCTV?'

Marshall looked around the rest of the garage. There were old boxes and scattered remnants of food, evidence that it was used by the homeless.

'Who do we ignore everyday?'

Biggs looked confused. 'I don't know. Is this some kind of riddle?'

She shook her head. 'The tramps, the bin raiders and the drunks. They're invisible, we all look the other way.'

'Fuck!'

'Let's go back over the tapes.'

18

SATURDAY

Wood Street Police Station, London. Saturday, November 30. 07:30

The city was eerily quiet as she ran. It was like something out of a movie, as if the entire population had been wiped out in a global epidemic.

She discovered her gym kit at the bottom of a box labelled 'Bedroom', not one of her finest organisational moments, but it meant there was one less box to deal with.

It felt good to get out in the fresh air, before the traffic pollution got too toxic, while the city still felt clean. The route along the river was cold, but she enjoyed the icy chill on her face, it helped blow away the cobwebs.

As her mind cleared, she played back the sequence of events. Melanie was waiting in the bar, received a text from her lover and headed for the restaurant that was less than five minutes away. Her lover had been told to meet in a different location. Which means that the killer knew not just about their affair, but had cloned both of their phones and sent them off in different directions.

When they got back to the office Biggs quickly identified the two shambling figures stumbling out of the car park and into the grounds of the church at 23:30. Ignored by the passers-by, the man held the woman around the waist, lurching across the road as if they were paralytic. Both were dressed in layers of old clothes and wore scraggy old wigs so that it was impossible to see their faces.

The van's plates had been stolen, but the vehicle identification number on the chassis was traced back to a Polish builder in Slough. Forensics had taken it back for further investigation but she wasn't going to get her hopes up.

He must have known her. Marshall thought, coming to the bridge at Limehouse Ship Lock. *But what was the motive? Why the marks on her feet?*

She slowed down to a walk, and took a drink of water. The route to the station was just over five miles and she had just hit the halfway point. Even on the cold wintry morning she was still sweating, not a good sign for someone who used to be able to run a 10K in under an hour.

Stretching out the twinges in her calves against one of the railings, she watched the narrow boats being manoeuvred around the Limehouse Basin. It reminded her of the ones she used to see on the canals on the outskirts of Bath. They were always filled with the most eccentric characters. Her old boyfriend, Will, used to call them 'river gypsies'.

Back then, Marshall had wondered what it would be like to simply take a boat and go, not caring where you would end up. There was something quite mystical about the canal people, they were drifters, nomads living off the grid, beyond the rules of the rest of society.

The killer seemed to have the same approach, staying in the shadows, making him harder to identify.

Picking up the pace she turned away from the river and

headed in towards Shadwell. Whatever the rationale behind the murder, she knew it had something to do with the symbols, she just didn't understand what they were trying to tell her yet.

19

SUNDAYS

Chiswick. Sunday, December 1. 12:00

'Hi Mum,' Marshall called out, closing the front door and kicking off her shoes.

There was always a certain smell when she walked into her parents' house. It was a combination of roast dinners, Lily of the Valley and furniture polish. Will had nicknamed it 'L'essence du home'. He was the only guy that could make her mother laugh and she treated him like the son she never had. He could do no wrong in her eyes. It probably would have been a different story if she had ever found out what they got up to under her clean cotton sheets. It still made Marshall smile to think of him laying naked in her bedroom, a lean seventeen-year-old with short curly hair and that cocky grin that she could never get enough of.

'In here love,' came the usual reply. 'Just giving your father his tea.'

Marshall took off her jacket and hung it on the newel post. Her mother hated to see her in a suit; it reminded her of what her only child did for a living. She always hated the idea of Marshall putting herself in danger every day.

The lounge was a shrine to the last thirty years. Framed photographs of their family adventures lined the sideboard, window sills and shelves. Happier times on holiday in Cornwall, Wales and the Lakes; weddings and birthdays, aunts and uncles — each one carefully labelled with a post-it note of their names written out in capital letters.

It was a form of remembering for her father, the dementia was eroding his brain. Wiping out sixty years of his life in a slow agonising way that those around him had to endure. There was no cure, no way to bring them back. So her mother had taken to keeping them alive through her photos.

There were old albums stacked on the side table. Marshall knew her mother spent hours every day going through them, crying silently to herself as he asked who the various people were.

Sitting in his chair by the patio doors, her father seemed to have aged considerably in the last few years. His irrepressible vitality had shrivelled as his condition worsened until he became just a shell of the man she loved. It was torture to see him in such a state, but she came to see them religiously, every Sunday, knowing that one day she wouldn't be able to and then she would miss it.

'Hi dad,' she said, kissing him gently on the cheek.

His eyes were glazed as he sat staring out into the garden.

'Hello Pip, nice to see you,' his mother prompted.

Her father turned his face up to her and smiled, the kind of smile that shone through his eyes.

Recognition, she thought, smiling back. *Today was going to be a good day.*

20

DEREK

Monument, London. Monday, December 2. 18:30

He can tell that Derek Reynolds hates the rain. The way the man's mouth twists as he pulls the collar of his raincoat up around his ears. How his shoulders hunch when he walks out into the street.

Water is life, he thinks to himself, watching Reynolds join the thousands of commuters huddling under umbrellas marching down Lower Thames Street.

He joins the masses, allowing himself to be carried along in their swarm. They are like an endless shoal of grey fish swimming up a river of drudgery. He studies their ashen expressions, feeling their soulless dead eyes staring straight through him. *I am a shade in the world of undead*, he thinks. *A lost soul wandering through the mire of human misery*.

The words of the sacred tablet echo through his mind.

'Separate thou the earth from the fire,
the subtle from the gross.'

. . .

Derek turns a corner into Pudding Lane.

Into the way of the Great Fire.

21

MONUMENT

Monument, London. Tuesday, December 3. 08:00

Rain was falling in sheets when Marshall came up out of Monument tube and headed directly into the nearest Starbucks.

She joined the end of a long queue of half-asleep, city-types busily scrolling through the morning's gossip on their phones. The smell of the freshly ground coffee awoke her addiction, and she was relieved to see that Biggs was already at the counter with two large lattes to go.

'You took your time,' he said, offering her one of the coffees.

Tying her wet hair back into a pony tail, she grabbed a napkin and dried the back of her neck before the water ran under the collar of her shirt.

'Jumper shutdown the Jubilee,' she said taking the cup and opening the lid to take a sip. 'Had to take the DLR.'

They went downstairs and found an empty booth. Marshall emptied four sachets of sugar into her drink. She needed the energy, her hangover was only just beginning to kick in.

'Have you got any paracetamol?' she asked, rubbing her eyes.

He opened his bag and pulled out a blister pack.

This was one of the reasons they nicknamed him 'Boy Scout' at the station, he was prepared for anything.

'Good day off?'

Marshall had stayed over in Chiswick until Monday, spending time with her dad, reminiscing about the good old days. Her mother had some documents she needed to sign, power of attorney and other legal crap which meant she didn't leave their house until late in the afternoon. By the time she got back to her flat there was hardly any daylight left and there was nothing left to eat in the fridge.

There weren't many places to eat around Island Gardens: a couple of pubs, a curry house and a Thai restaurant. She could have gone through the foot tunnel to Greenwich, but it was getting dark and she couldn't be bothered. She opted for a takeout from the Thai who, more importantly, delivered wine if you paid in cash.

James used to complain about how much she would drink while she was working a case. She would ignore him, sitting up late into the night poring over the details on her laptop. She never really paid him that much attention at the time. He usually gave up after the first bottle and by the time she was into the second, he had already gone to bed.

It was strange how she missed the nagging. Somehow wine didn't quite taste as good when she could drink as much as she wanted.

. . .

Marshall dropped the tablets into her mouth and swallowed them dry.

'What've we got so far?'

Biggs pulled out his notebook. 'Fire service were called to Monument at four o'clock this morning. One of the heat sensors went off.'

'Someone set fire to the Monument. That's ironic.'

'Someone set fire to someone in the Monument.'

'Ah. I see. Shouldn't we be going?'

'No rush. Forensics are in there now. It's a small space, a basement underneath the ticket office.'

'Who's attending? Gates?'

Biggs nodded. 'Counter Terrorism have most of the square cordoned off. Wouldn't let him near it until the bomb squad gave it the all clear. They thought it might have been an incendiary.'

'Bet he didn't take too kindly to that.'

The detective constable smiled. 'No. Salazar had to come down and sort it out. You can imagine how much she enjoyed that.'

'The original Olympic torch.'

He smiled. 'Never goes out.'

'So she's running the show?'

Biggs shook his head. 'She hung around long enough to make friends with the CT commander and then bailed. She was asking where you were. I told her you had to go to the docs.'

'Thanks,' Marshall said with a grimace. *Another black mark*. 'So do we know who the vic is?'

'Apparently the body is too badly burned. They think it's male, but we're probably going to be working with dental records on this one.'

Tasting the coffee, Marshall winced, grabbing a wooden stick and stirring it vigorously.

'You're going to love this,' he said, taking out his phone. 'Gates sent me it ten minutes ago.'

The image on the phone was hard to process at first. It was a shiny black surface that looked like the carapace of a beetle, and in the middle of the screen were two more alchemical symbols, outlined in pink unburned skin.

'Fuck,' Marshall said, her caffeine-fuelled brain finally beginning to function.

'Looks like we might have another one.'

The square around Monument was cordoned off. Fire engines blocked Pudding Lane and Monument Street and a crowd of onlookers were gathering in Fish Street Hill, held back by a line of uniformed officers.

Marshall and Biggs worked their way to the front. The press were hounding the stony-faced PCs, trying to get a decent shot of the scene. They turned on Marshall as she flashed her warrant card at a sergeant, firing questions at her while she ducked under the tape. She ignored them and they turned on Biggs who followed quickly behind. Weaving between the incident response vehicles they reached the column.

The weathered stone of the base was scorched with soot. The SOCO team were waiting beside the narrow entrance, their cases of equipment stacked against the iron railings.

Suddenly, a man backed out of the doorway, carrying one end of a body bag. It was a tight fit, a second man appeared holding the other end.

It's a strange shape, Marshall thought, watching the men place it carefully into the back of a black van.

Marshall spotted Gates standing talking to the fire commander and went over to him.

'The thing is Portland stone.' She overheard him say. 'The temperature in there was nowhere near hot enough to crack it, let alone damage the foundations.'

She waited patiently until the conversation ended.

'Marshall,' he greeted her with a look of frustration. 'Are you claustrophobic?'

'Don't think so.'

'I am. It's a bloody nightmare down there. Not quite sure what Wren was thinking of when he designed that basement.'

The entrance to the underground space was a small trapdoor. Marshall had to twist her body as she descended the stone steps.

Gates was right about the space, it was a tiny room with a domed ceiling. There was hardly any light. In the semi-darkness she could see a small circular hole in the roof directly under the centre of the spiral staircase.

Switching on the torch the pathologist had given her, she scanned the room. Its narrow beam finding nothing but blackened stone, it was like a cell in a medieval dungeon. There was a strange smell, Marshall had dealt with a few arsons in her time on the beat. Mostly domestic house fires, they smelled of charred wood or the foam of the furniture. This was different, she was expecting burned meat, but this had a chemical tang.

She tried to imagine how the victim was dragged down those stairs. They would have to have been drugged, there was no way that the killer would have been able to get a fully-conscious man into this place — it would have taken too long and they would have been struggling the whole way.

Unless they knew the killer.

22

WORK

Wood Street Station, London. Tuesday, December 3. 14:00

'The cameras around Monument were disabled at approximately nine last night,' Donovan read aloud from the report, standing in the centre of the incident room. Images of the victim's burned body and shots of the crime scene were looping on the plasma screen behind him.

'It rained heavily last night, so there's little chance of getting any physical evidence from exterior. No ID on the victim as yet, but Gates is hopeful for dental. Although apparently the heat has cracked the enamel of most of the victim's teeth.'

'All his fillings melted,' Devlin whispered to Marshall, leaning in so close she could smell his aftershave. Not that he shaved, he had a permanent five o'clock shadow. It was masking a multitude of other scents, and coupled with the fact that he was still wearing the shirt from yesterday, she assumed he got lucky last night.

Donovan scowled, crossing his arms over his large stomach. 'You wish to add something DS Devlin?'

'No sir.'

'Then shut the fuck up,' he snapped, turning to the screen and enlarging one of the photos. 'So far the only clue we've got are those bloody symbols. Looks like we've got another victim but a different MO. Have we got anything on the first set?'

'They're old,' Biggs said, standing up. 'Ancient cyphers for sulphur and air.'

Donovan looked blankly at him. 'Which means?'

The constable flicked nervously back and forth through his notebook and then shrugged. 'Nothing so far, sorry Guv.'

'Jesus wept, then find someone who does! Do you want me to wipe your arse for you as well?'

Sitting back down, Biggs's cheeks flushed crimson as he started searching on the internet. Marshall felt his pain. They had all made the mistake of admitting they didn't know something to the DCI. *You only do it once*, she thought to herself.

The Chief Inspector rubbed his chin, reminding himself he too hadn't shaved for a couple of days. Donovan had the hang-dog look of a man whose wife had kicked him out for the last time. This was the kind of case that could quickly get under your skin, keeping you awake at night. There were dark shadows under his puffy eyes and his grey hair was messed up, like he'd slept on someone's sofa.

'Any ideas on how the killer got in? Or disabled the CCTV?' Marshall asked.

Again there was an awkward silence, a collective shrug.

'As good a place to start as any,' Donovan agreed. 'Devlin you stay on the first victim. Marshall, I want you to concentrate on this one. Get yourself down to control and find out what happened to the cameras.'

23

CAMERAS

Wood Street Station, London. Tuesday, December 3. 16:00

Multiple views of Monument Square were playing back on the bank of monitors. Grey scenes of commuters making their way through the pouring rain, their faces obscured by hats, umbrellas and folded newspapers.

'Can you speed it up?' Marshall asked the operator.

He nodded and tapped his keyboard.

The streets quickly drained of people. By seven o'clock the square was empty apart from a few stragglers and then at eight the screens went dark.

'How long does this go on for?'

'Five hours.'

'And they all went out?'

'Every single one that covers the square.'

She looked at the dark screens. 'How can that happen?'

The operator sighed, folding his arms and leaning back in his chair. 'Either they hacked into our system and wiped the data, which is unlikely, it's encrypted and backed up to a private cloud, or they disrupted the network.'

'How?'

'All the cameras are IP based, they are accessible through a thin client, but you would have to know how. It would take someone with knowledge of our security systems to get into it.'

Or Secret Services, Marshall considered.

'Can you go back to five-thirty? When the ticket office closed.'

They scrubbed back and forth along the timeline for over an hour, looking for the smallest detail in the grainy images. Her eyes ached from concentrating too hard on the harsh screen. There was nothing. The homeless didn't appear until after ten and none of them made any attempt to go near the entrance.

He's a ghost, she said to herself, leaving the control room. *Two murders and no real evidence.*

There was a basic rule of forensics called "Locard's Exchange Principle". It states that the perpetrator of a crime will always leave something behind at the scene, and they will also take something away from it. Marshall liked the theory and in most of her cases it had been proven correct, leading to a conviction.

To have such a total lack of evidence was a clue in its own right. It meant that the killer was careful, that they knew how to destroy or ensure that nothing of their presence was left at the scene. That meant he had a good understanding of forensics, and now it seems security systems as well.

Is he one of us? She wondered.

It was a hard thing to contemplate, the worst of all scenarios, a killer cop.

24

MORTUARY

Westminster Mortuary, London. Wednesday, December 4. 09:00

Gates hadn't started his examination when Marshall turned up the next morning. The receptionist told her that he had only just arrived and was still preparing the lab.

She knew that was a polite warning, but went down all the same. She knew from her days at the Met that Gates was like a bear with a sore head before his second coffee — which is why she always brought one.

The corpse was a blackened husk, curled into the foetus position like something from Pompeii. It was hardly recognisable as a person, more like some kind of overgrown insect.

The pathologist was sitting on a metal stool beside the table, a pair of headphones hanging from his ears. Humming along to a Beatles track, he carefully took skin samples from the body. He was in his mid-sixties and had 'let himself go' as her mother would say. His grey, wiry hair hadn't seen a barber in six months and his beard needed a trim. He reminded Marshall of a homeless Santa, but his one redeeming feature was that he could read a corpse like a book.

His assistants were carefully avoiding him, preparing trolleys with the usual array of vicious-looking tools and setting up the recording equipment.

Marshall handed him the coffee.

'Much appreciated,' Gates mumbled, pulling out his headphones and blowing on the steaming black liquid.

She walked around the table.

'Male or female?'

'Male. The pelvic girdle is too narrow for a female.'

'Was he tied?' Marshall asked, staring at the hands, the fingers interlocked as if he was begging.

The pathologist nodded. 'There are ligature marks on ankle and wrist that show he was bound.'

'Not barbed wire?'

'My guess would be cable ties, the heat of the fire vaporised the plastic.'

'Fuck! What happened to his eyes?' she said, staring at the dark, gaping holes.

'At first, I wondered if they'd melted. Usually with burn victims the lids are sealed shut, it's a natural response — involuntary. In this case I believe the eyes were removed before he was set alight.'

Marshall tried not to imagine what the killer had used to take out the man's eyes. The image of Melanie's mouth resurfaced and she knew it would have been painful.

'Do you know what was used?'

Gates shook his head and took a sip of the coffee. 'Robusta?'

She smiled, it was a test, he was something of a snob when it came to coffee beans. 'Arabica.'

'You spoil me.'

Marshall noticed a strange smell emanating from the body. Beneath the sharp tang of burned meat there was something that reminded her of an old heater her grandfather used to keep in his greenhouse.

'What did he use? Paraffin?'

Gates leaned in to sniff the body. 'Smells more like ethanol rather than kerosene. Whatever it was, it burned so hot that it melted his fillings and cracked the enamel.'

The lips were peeled back and the skin contracted so that it looked as if he were smiling. Gold glimmered from between the blackened teeth.

'Are you going to be able to get anything for dental?'

He nodded to one of the machines the assistant was wheeling in. 'We'll start with x-rays, should give us something to work with.' Then picking up a drill, he added. 'Otherwise I can try and extract some DNA from the dentine.'

Across the seared back of the victim, the two symbols stood out in pale white flesh. Marshall studied them closely, the lines were near perfect as if they had been stencilled.

'Do you know how he protected the skin?' she asked, pulling out her phone and taking a series of photographs.

With some effort Gates pushed himself up off the stool and walked around to join her.

'My guess would be that he used some form of flame-retardant gel. A superabsorbent polymer, like the ones that stunt men use in fire scenes. Whoever this guy is, he certainly knows his chemistry. These are not high street materials. Any idea what they mean?'

Marshall checked the images before attaching them to an email to Biggs.

'They're alchemical symbols. The ones on the first victim were air and sulphur. My DC has found an expert at King's. We're seeing him this morning.' She looked at the time on her phone. 'Which means I have to go. Let me know what you find on the x-rays'.

'Of course.' Gates put his headphones back in. 'Thanks for the coffee.'

25

KING'S COLLEGE

King's College, London. Wednesday, December 4. 11:00

Biggs was waiting for Marshall at the Strand entrance to the university. He looked as if he could have just come out of a lecture.

'Did Gates manage to get anything from dental?'

Marshall shook her head. 'Too early to tell, the teeth are fused together.'

Biggs instinctively flexed his jaw at the thought of it. 'Fuck.'

'Did you print out the symbols?'

He nodded, tapping the leather satchel hanging from his shoulder.

'Good, don't show him the crime scene photos, and no mention of the murders,' she warned, walking under the arch and onto the campus. 'Who is this guy anyway?'

Biggs followed, taking out his notebook. 'Michael Gresham, Professor of Medieval Studies at King's. He's also a research fellow in History and Philosophy at Oxford and wrote his doctorate on the history of early modern magic and science. His bio says that he "focuses on the confluence of learned magic, science and religion in early modern Europe".'

Sounds like a party animal, Marshall thought, having visions of some grey, dusty old librarian.

The professor was in the middle of a lecture when they finally found him. They sneaked quietly through the doors, taking seats on a bench at the back of the auditorium like tardy students.

He was not what Marshall was expecting. In his mid-forties, he had a beard and dark hair shot through with streaks of grey. A pair of thick-rimmed black glasses gave him the air of an archetypal academic.

Projected onto the large screen behind him was a medieval illustration of a witch being tortured. His voice was clear and deep as he continued his lecture.

'...which brings us to the *Malleus Maleficarum*, or "Hammer of Witches", possibly the best known treatise on witchcraft of the time, published in 1487 by the discredited Catholic clergyman Heinrich Kramer. It endorses extermination of witches and develops a detailed legal and theological theory for this purpose.'

The slide changed to show another illustration of a burning woman.

'The *Malleus* elevated sorcery to the criminal status of heresy and prescribed inquisitorial practices for secular courts in order to eliminate witches. The procedures included torture to obtain confessions and the death penalty as a remedy against the evils of witchcraft. During this period it was typical to burn heretics alive at the stake and the *Malleus* encouraged the same treatment of witches.

Burning was seen as a way to ensure that the body could not be resurrected on Judgement Day.'

Marshall nudged Biggs in the ribs, signalling to him to note that down.

The professor stepped out from behind the lectern.

'Your assignment over the Christmas break will be to study the Pendle Witch Trials of 1612.'

The house lights came up and the students filed past towards the exit, eyeing the two of them with suspicion. Marshall tried to remember what it was like to be that young and full of hope. Her dreams of university had died with Will, she decided to join the police the day after his funeral.

'Can I help you?' The professor's microphone was still on and his voice echoed around the now empty auditorium.

They walked down to the lectern and showed their warrant cards.

'Her Majesty's Constabulary,' he said with a mocking bow. 'How may I be of assistance?'

Marshall thought there was a certain arrogance about him. An air of superiority that certain academics acquired, as if they knew the secrets of the universe. Her old sergeant would have called him a 'ponce', but there were rules about that kind of thing these days.

'We were wondering if you might be able to help us with these,' Biggs said, holding up prints of the symbols that he had downloaded from a website.

Taking off his glasses, Gresham's brown eyes widened slightly as he studied the pictures. Chewing one arm of his spectacles, he examined each in turn.

. . .

'Sulphur and mercury,' he said, holding up the relevant symbols. 'Aristotle's smoke and vapour. The other two are elements: fire and air.'

'Aristotle?' Marshall repeated.

'Alchemists believed that all other metals were formed from combinations of these two. In order to create the noble metals, like gold, you would have to find the perfect blend of mercury and sulphur. An eighth-century Arabian chemist by the name of Jabir documented it in his *Book of Clarification*.'

Biggs scribbled down the name of the book, but Marshall was failing to see how it was relevant to the case.

'What does it mean?' she asked, tapping on mercury.

He frowned, putting his glasses back on. 'You have to understand that alchemy is a complex, symbolic science. Mercury, or quicksilver as it was known then, was revered for its ability to transcend both liquid and solid states, or life and death. It is often represented as a serpent. It's also one of the seven alchemical metals, and a planet of course.'

'And sulphur?'

He sighed, holding up the second image. 'Sulphur represents evaporation or dissolution. The fluid between high and low, along with mercury and salt it makes up *Tria Prima* of alchemy. It's all part of the purification process known as *Solve et Coagula*.'

Marshall was beginning to resent the way he spoke to her, condescending and offhand, like a student who didn't really understand the question she was asking. She found herself biting her bottom lip, it was a habit that her mother had never managed to drum out of her. 'Do people still practice alchemy?' Biggs asked, filling the awkward silence.

The professor laughed and spread his hands. 'Everyday. Aren't we all in search of the divine?'

'He meant are there those who still believe in this,' she snapped, pointing at the symbols and trying to hold her frustration in check. The man's attitude was irritating to the point of annoying.

'That depends,' Gresham said more seriously. 'Transmutation of the base metals into gold. No, modern chemistry has proved beyond a doubt that it's not possible. As for the philosopher's stone — the pursuit of eternal life, I think that now lies in the hands of the cosmetics industry and perhaps genomics. But as for the old maxim: As above, so below, there are still many who believe that the planets are influencing our fates.'

Astrology? Marshall wondered if this was becoming a total waste of time.

'Were alchemists ever tortured?' Biggs asked pointing at the screen. 'Like the witches.'

Good question. Marshall thought, unsure what it was about this guy that was throwing her off her game.

The professor handed back the print-outs. 'They were proto-scientists. Many were accomplished scholars. Although the transmutation of base metals did attract its fair share of charlatans or "puffers" as they were called. Some were imprisoned, mostly for fraud. One Italian swindler by the name of Cajetani was hung from a golden gallows because he cheated so many of their money.'

'And they never experimented on people?' Marshall asked.

Gresham studied her intensely, as if seeing her for the first time. 'Quite the opposite actually. Paracelsus was searching for a panacea, a medicine capable of curing all diseases, that would rid the body of all impurities.'

'So they were doctors?'

He folded his arms. 'The lines between magic and

science weren't so clearly drawn in those days. Simon Forman was said to have healed himself of the plague during Shakespeare's time. He developed a thriving practice as an astrologer physician. Although after his death many decried him as an evil magician in league with the devil.'

Biggs glanced at Marshall. She could see that he too was running out of patience with the man.

Gresham turned and went over to the lectern. 'I must admit that I am intrigued with your line of questioning. Two detectives asking about alchemical practices leads me towards one conclusion: you're investigating a murder if not two.'

'We cannot comment on that at the moment,' Marshall replied, impressed with his insight.

The professor continued undeterred by her answer. 'Of course you can't, but my guess is that the murderer left those marks on the body?'

'I'm afraid we cannot say, it's an ongoing case.'

'I understand,' he said, picking up his notebook. 'But if I'm not mistaken there is a least one more victim to come.'

He drew a near-perfect circle and then put a horizontal line through the middle. 'Salt.'

26

HOLMES

Wood Street Station, London. Wednesday, December 4. 15:00

Marshall hated computers.

There were only a few things in her life that she couldn't master. She could speak French, play the guitar, ride a motorbike and gained a black-belt in Jujitsu. At school, she was one of those annoying kids that always knew the answer. Her hand would shoot up before any of the others. She liked learning, she was good at it.

But computers were her nemesis.

This was not true of all technology; phones and tablets were fine, but there was something about a PC that brought her out in a cold sweat.

It was not the machine itself, but the software that ran on it which was obviously designed by someone who never actually had to use it. Things were always in the wrong places and unless you knew exactly what you were searching for it seemed impossible to find the answers.

While others hated the idea of artificial intelligence, she couldn't wait for the day when you could simply ask a question and get the right answer. James had bought her an Amazon Echo for Christmas the year before and they had spent a hilarious evening trying to get it to answer questions from Trivial Pursuit.

She opened up her laptop, logged into HOLMES and started a search for murders involving symbols in the last ten years.

There was nothing.

Opening a new browser window, she typed the same search terms into Google.

Zodiac killer evaded police for 50 years.

The words sat above a grid of images, some were of circles with crosses through them, others were made from the letters 'BTK' or pentagrams.

Clicking on the first search result, the screen refreshed to show a page dedicated to the Zodiac killings. The article described in graphic detail the five murders in Northern California during the late sixties. The killer had apparently sent a series of cryptographic letters to the police, claiming to have killed thirty-seven people. He continued to taunt the police into the seventies before disappearing altogether.

She clicked back to the search results and read a few of the others. There were a lot of Americans, many of whom were motivated by some deep psychological need to be caught. The symbols were like a calling card and in most cases except for the Zodiac, it had eventually led to their arrest. They wanted to make sure they were recognised for their work, like an artist signing a painting — it was a form of ownership.

Marshall didn't need a professor to work out that the murderer was making some kind of statement. Both victims' bodies had been mutilated in unusual and sadistic ways. They were being punished for something — she just couldn't work out what it was yet. For Marshall it was just like trying to learn a new language. She had to find a way to decode the messages the killer left behind.

She cleared the search and looked up the professor.

His bio was extensive. He had published three books and collaborated on a dozen more. There were excerpts from Oxford and Cambridge websites as well as more than one appearance on the BBC podcast 'In Our Time' with Melvyn Bragg. She skimmed through the academic headlines until she found something more interesting about his personal life.

"Professor reprimanded over student affair."

Intrigued, Marshall opened the article to find a story from one of the red-tops, the sleazy end of the news, detailing how Gresham had been accused of sleeping with one of his female students.

He denied the allegation, but the paper published it all the same. The student in question was shown beside him at a garden party in Oxford. The professor was at least ten years younger, he looked like a movie star, with sunglasses and a half-open shirt. His hand was around the woman's waist. She was smiling at the camera.

The article went on to describe how the nineteen-year-old was accusing him of raping her during one of their tutorial sessions.

He was suspended while the matter was investigated.

Marshall typed his name into HOLMES. There was one

result for speeding back in the early nineties but other than that he was clean.

She went back to Google and switched to an image search. An array of photographs lined up across the screen. There was no denying he was a handsome man, but there was something about him that disturbed her, she couldn't put her finger on what it was.

Could he be the killer? She thought to herself staring at one of his more recent images. *Could he be that arrogant?*

Pushing the idea to the back of her mind, Marshall printed out a few of the links from his bio. They were long articles on the history of alchemy and she sat back in her chair and began to read.

27

INCIDENT ROOM

Wood Street Police Station, London. Thursday, December 5. 09:00

'So we're looking for a chemist?' Donovan asked, trying to hide the sarcasm and failing.

'An *alchemist*,' Marshall corrected him. 'Probably an academic.'

'Like your nutty professor?'

'Gresham has a solid alibi,' Biggs interrupted. 'He was speaking at a college dinner on the night of the first murder.'

'And the second?'

Biggs checked through his notes. 'Watching "Measure for Measure" at the Globe theatre with his students. Some kind of university field trip.'

'How very cultural,' growled the detective chief inspector.

'Gates's report confirms that the chemicals used in the fire were not widely available. I've got Baxter checking the suppliers,' Marshall added, knowing how the DCI hated dead ends.

Donovan nodded. 'Good. Did you ask about the significance of the tongue and the eyes?'

'No, Gresham guessed it was a murder inquiry, and I didn't think it was wise to share all the details,' she replied.

'You did the right thing. I want a total media blackout. Salazar's downstairs with the press office right now. The fire at Monument made the six o'clock news. The press is already sniffing around.'

'Gates thinks the eyes were taken out before he died.'

Donovan winced, subconsciously rubbing his own puffy lids in the process. 'He's taking trophies, that's not a good sign.'

She knew what he was thinking, that they were serial killings, but neither wanted to say the word out loud, it was too early. The protocol for a serial was three murders and it came with a heavy price. Her boss was never a great one for finances. Their budgets were being cut every year and she could see the look of dread in his eyes at the cost of running such an extensive investigation.

'Okay,' he said, clapping his hands together. 'Biggs go back over the footage again. See if we're missing something earlier. Maybe he paid it a visit in the days before the incident. Took some photos of the cameras before he knocked them out. Also check with control on who has access to their systems. Marshall come with me.'

Biggs nodded and left.

Marshall followed him into his office and Donovan closed the door.

'I realise we haven't talked about your promotion since you came back.'

'It's been a bit hectic.'

The DCI motioned for her to sit.

'Do you still want to go for it?'

Marshall nodded, trying not to look too enthusiastic. 'Yes, but what about Salazar?'

Donovan flinched at the sound of her name. 'Acting Detective Inspector Salazar has also expressed an interest in making the position permanent.'

He's not so keen.

'Off the record Guv?'

He smiled. 'Off the record. I will give you every opportunity to run this investigation. You're the best detective in the department. Bring this one in and the post is yours, just make sure she doesn't steal your thunder.'

Inwardly, she smiled. They both knew Salazar would be a challenge, but she could handle her. 'Thank you, sir.'

Baxter knocked on the door.

Donovan waved him in.

'Sorry Guv, but there's a Professor Gresham downstairs, asking to speak to DS Marshall.'

The inspector turned to her. 'It seems you've got yourself an admirer,' he said with a wink. 'Better go and see what he wants.'

28

PROFESSOR

Interview Room 3. Wood Street Police Station. Thursday, December 5. 09:30

Gresham wore a tweed jacket and a black polo neck sweater. His beard was short and neatly trimmed and his hair was swept back, as if he had just stepped out of the pages of GQ magazine.

Opening the door to the interview room, Marshall caught the scent of his aftershave, it smelt expensive.

He stood as she entered, like a perfect gentleman, offering his hand. 'DS Marshall, thank you for seeing me.'

She took it and felt his strong grip as they shook.

'No problem, how can I help you?'

He smiled, taking his seat once more. 'I think it's more how I can help you,' he replied without a hint of his usual arrogance. 'I saw the news last night, the fire at Monument. I take it that is where you found the second body?'

Marshall paused, unsure of how much to tell him. Something in her gut told her to take a chance. 'It was.

Although I would prefer if you didn't mention anything to the press.'

He looked a little shocked. 'No. Never.'

She remembered the article about the student, the media had not been kind to him back then. He was very unlikely to bring that on himself again.

'So how do you think you can assist us?'

He sat back in his chair, taking out a tattered old notebook. 'You'll have to excuse me, my memory is not what it was and I want to make sure I have this right. Aren't you going to record this?'

Marshall looked puzzled. 'Do you think I need to?'

'I would rather not have to repeat myself.'

She turned on the machine and waited for the tone. 'This is DS Marshall, the date is Thursday, 5th of December, 2019. Present is Professor Michael Gresham, King's College. Commencing witness statement.'

He cleared his throat while the tone played out on the tape recorder.

'The Monument was designed by Christoper Wren and Robert Hooke to memorialise the Great Fire of 1666. Completed in 1677 its single Doric column stands over one-hundred feet high.'

'Are you here to give me a history lesson Professor?' Marshall interrupted.

'No, sorry, it's force of habit. The men who designed the column were both members of the Royal Society. A group of scientists and inventors whose membership included Sir Isaac Newton, Robert Boyle and many other aspiring academics. When they built Monument, they created more than just a towering pillar, it's also a scientific instrument; a zenith telescope — for gravity and pendulum experiments.

There is an underground laboratory beneath the ticket booth for observers.

'Which is where we found the body.'

His eyes widened slightly. 'I was about to ask.'

'Why do you think he chose that particular place?'

'I can't speak to his motives, only that the members of the Royal Society were fascinated with alchemy. Newton wrote many treatises on the subject.'

'It was a telescope?'

'A zenith telescope. The central shaft can be used for precise measurements of the stars.'

'That may be relevant.'

'Why?'

'Because the victim had his eyes removed.'

She took his details, and escorted him out of the building. Marshall had a feeling that she was going to need his help again, and the thought of having to put up with his annoying arrogance wasn't something she was looking forward to.

29

PARNELL

Wood Street Police Station, London. Thursday, December 5. 10:30

Devlin was making himself a coffee when Marshall came back up to the incident room. He looked unusually happy to see her. There was a gleam in his eye that was normally reserved for new female recruits.

'Your bloke works in financial crime doesn't he?'

'NCA. Financial intelligence unit,' she corrected him, ignoring the fact that James probably wasn't her bloke anymore.

Devlin shrugged. 'Same shit, different name. Do you think you can get him to run a trace on the Galeta Group for me? I'm getting fucking nowhere. It was registered by a law firm in Panama for a private client and they're not willing to share any details.'

He walked over to his desk and picked up a sheet of paper. There were a series of company names on it with bank swift codes, most of which had been crossed out.

'He's very busy,' she said, trying to think of a better

excuse not to have to phone him. She didn't want to admit to Devlin that they had split up. It would be around the station in minutes if he found out.

He seemed to smile with his eyes, she could see how the ladies would fall for it. 'It's a five minute job. They have access to international stuff that we can't get anywhere near.'

Marshall was struggling to say no. He was right. James would be able to follow the trail back to the source. He was brilliant at tracing financial anomalies. They used to joke that in another life he could have made a fortune as a hedge fund manager for the mafia, he knew all the ways to make money disappear.

She took her phone out and snapped a shot of the notes. 'I'll ask him tonight,' she lied.

Devlin looked relieved. 'Thanks. Beers on me.'

She nodded and went back to her desk. Biggs was reviewing the CCTV from Monument just before the incident.

'Anything?' Marshall asked, hoping she hadn't missed something.

He stopped the playback on a view of the square around the column which was filled with umbrellas. 'The last admission was at five. It's shut by five-thirty. The last to leave was a member of staff at five forty-five. The CCTV cuts out around eight.'

He fast forwarded the footage through the next few hours until the signal from the feeds scrambled and went dark.

'So?'

Biggs spun round in his chair to face her. 'Either he already had the victim in the basement before they closed, or he kept him somewhere nearby until everyone had left.'

'And he had keys.'

'No sign of a forced entry.'

Marshall grabbed her coat. 'Call the manager. I want to take another look.'

Monument Square seemed much larger now that all of the ambulances and fire engines had gone. It never ceased to surprise Marshall how quickly life returned to normal.

The ticket office manager hovered by the entrance which was still shrouded in police tape. He was a tall, gaunt-faced man called Parnell. His dark eyes were magnified by the thick lenses in his glasses and Marshall tried hard not to stare at the long wisps of hair that shifted around in the breeze over his balding head.

'Mr Parnell,' Biggs said, showing his warrant card. 'I'm DC Biggs, this is DS Marshall.'

The man looked genuinely pleased to see them, as if this was the most interesting thing that had ever happened in his life.

'I've brought the staff roster as you requested,' he said proudly, handing a manila folder to Biggs. 'For the last month.'

Marshall stared at the blackened stonework and the secure metal grille that had been bolted across it. 'Who has keys to this?' she asked, pointing at the old lock.

'Three of us,' Parnell said, taking out a large ring of keys and showing her a worn iron key. 'It's over a hundred years old,' he added proudly.

'And the others all have theirs?'

'As far as I am aware,' he replied, but there was a pause that told Marshall that he didn't know for sure.

Biggs opened the roster. 'Can you tell me who they are?'

Parnell gave him their names and Biggs underlined each one.

'Is there any other way to access the office?'

The manager laughed. 'I'm afraid Wren didn't go much on health and safety. There's only one way in and out.'

Marshall looked around the square. *He would have stayed close*, she thought, *kept the victim quiet until the commuters had gone home.*

'What is that?' She said pointing at the large glass box sitting at one end of the square.

'Public toilets. It won an award.'

The rest of the square was made up of office buildings, bars and restaurants. There was nowhere else to hide a body.

'Can you think of anyone else who might have had access to the keys? A previous employee who might have made a copy?' Biggs asked.

The man's lips pursed together, as if he were about to whistle. Marshall was relieved when he didn't.

'There was that trouble with Mayberry. Not something we like to talk about, he wasn't a bad sort of chap. We caught him running private tours after hours. Had to let him go.'

'And do you still have his details?'

'I'd have to talk to HR, you know with GDPR and all that.'

'This is a murder investigation Mr Parnell.'

'Is it? I was told it was some kind of electrical fire.'

Bollocks.

'Was he badly burned?'

Marshall's phone rang, it was Salazar. *Baxter was right, she is a witch.*

'Where are you?'

'At Monument interviewing the manager about previous employees.'

'We've told the press it was an electrical fault.'

'Yeah, so I hear.' Marshall said, glaring at Biggs, who was still talking to the manager. 'Must have missed the memo on that one.'

'So did he give you anything useful?'

Marshall toyed with the idea of telling her about Mayberry, but decided against it. *Not until I've checked it out.*

'No, but we have a staff list to work through.'

'Good. We've got a match on the DNA Gates extracted from the teeth. The second victim was a twenty-eight year old male by the name of Derek Reynolds. He was Head of IT at Credit Suisse in Lower Thames Street. No next of kin. I'm getting a warrant to search his home. It's on the South Coast somewhere near Dover. I want you to go down and make sure that the locals don't fuck it up.'

30

LIGHTHOUSE

Friday, December 6. 05:30

Biggs had volunteered to drive, booking out one of the new BMW X5s from the car pool. It was still dark when he pulled up outside her flat, acting like a kid with a new toy. There was an irrepressible look of joy on his boyish face as she climbed in — one that made Marshall wonder how long it had been since he'd passed his test.

Getting out of the city before six in the morning was relatively easy. The residents of East London were still pouring milk onto their cereal as Biggs drove over Dartford bridge and into Kent.

Marshall was planning to catch up on some sleep for the first hour, but Biggs's choice of music and the double-shot latte he bought her managed to ruin any chances of a nap.

She wasn't a morning person. Caffeine was the only thing that made her even vaguely human. When she was a kid, her father had spent countless hours inventing new ways to wake her up, the worst of which was the dreaded cold flannel. Marshall liked sleep and she just seemed to need more than most other people. Will used to joke that it was because of her overly-large brain requiring more time to reboot. James used to call her a dormouse, that was the difference between the two of them.

After they passed Rochester she gave up trying to snooze and opened the case file for Reynolds.

'What does a Head of IT actually do?' she asked, turning down the music.

'It's a pretty generic job title,' Biggs replied, pulling out into the fast lane and accelerating hard. Marshall watched the needle of the speedometer creep towards 90mph.

'Some oversee networks or servers, infrastructure stuff, while others look after software. There's literally hundreds of different roles. My mate Trev calls himself a software architect, but in reality he's a developer for a gambling app. He just likes to big up his job title.'

'So could Reynolds have worked at Lloyd's at some point? On their systems?'

'Potentially. Baxter has requested his HR records from Credit Suisse. He says it's going to take a while, they work on Government contracts so it's a bit sensitive.'

'Twenty-eight, not married, no kids and no immediate relatives,' she read aloud, 'not much to work with.'

'He must have done something right. I Googled his place last night, it's a converted lighthouse, worth well over a million.'

Marshall flicked through the notes. Since Reynolds had only one conviction for possession, Biggs had scraped most of his profile from the web. Instagram images of the man snowboarding with a bunch of mates were pasted next to a bio that looked like it had been pulled from LinkedIn.

'He's got a degree in Computer Science, and a masters in

Cryptography,' Biggs said, saving her the bother of having to read it. Marshall was grateful, reading in the car made her feel sick. She was a terrible back-seat passenger, her parents always let her ride in the front seat ever since the time she threw up down the back of her father's neck while they were driving to Wales.

'Sounds like he would have been more at home at GCHQ.'

'Doesn't pay as well as the financial sector.'

'So you think he could have hacked the CCTV?'

Biggs slowed down and moved into the middle lane. 'I found a couple of tweets he made from DEFCON Vegas 2018.'

'What's that?'

'A hacker convention. They have speakers from the industry and cyber-security challenges where they try to hack into each others' servers — all white hat stuff. It's one of the biggest, the Ministry of Defence and FBI usually attend.'

'Sounds like a load of fun,' she said dryly, looking back at the notes. 'Doesn't say what happened to his family in here.'

'He was in and out of foster homes for most of his teens. Baxter was going to talk to social services about getting his files sent over.'

'So how come he can afford a lighthouse?'

'Made some good investments I guess. Maybe he got into bitcoin early.'

Approaching South Foreland, the horizon shifted and suddenly there was nothing but sky and sea as if the land had just been cut away. The sight of the coast was a welcome change from the two hours of never-ending green fields, although the dark clouds that gathered out over the water were threatening more rain.

Marshall could spot a cumulonimbus from miles away. She spent more than her fair share of family trips touring around the wetter parts of the British Isles. Her mother was not keen on flying and so most of their summer holidays were spent in caravans or camping in Wales and the Lake District. Every so often, the sun would bless them with its presence and they would pile into the VW camper and head down to the beach to surf, but mostly she would come back whiter than when she had left. Will used to call it her 'rain tan'.

The Victorian lighthouse overlooked the cliffs of Dover and the treacherous Goodwin Sands. It was a solid-looking white tower with crenelated battlements that surrounded the lantern room. A single-storey square building sat at its base. Marshall wondered what it would be like to stand up there on a stormy night. It was exactly the kind of place her dad would have dragged her around when he got bored of sitting on the beach.

The local police were already on the scene when they pulled up. They were wearing heavy coats and gloves and it wasn't until Marshall stepped out of the climate controlled BMW that she understood why: the wind howled around them carrying with it the scent of snow.

'DS Marshall?' The detective shouted over the gale. She nodded, holding out her hand. 'DI Wilkins?'

He shook it and then quickly stuck his hands back in his

pockets. The wind sliced through the thin jacket she had stupidly decided to wear. There was a warmer one on the back seat, but she didn't want to walk back and get it — *it would make me look weak.*

Wilkins was in his mid-fifties, with a jowly face of liverish grey where the cold had leeched all of the colour, all except for his radish nose.

No sign of forensics, she thought to herself. *Gates would have kittens if we went in before his team.*

'Shall we?' Wilkins said, handing her a pair of latex gloves and turning towards the lighthouse.

There was a Porsche 911 Turbo parked on the gravelled drive. Biggs took out his digital SLR and snapped a few shots of the car as they walked past.

Entering the ground floor of the outbuilding, Marshall was impressed how effective the thick old walls were against the weather. It was quiet and peaceful inside, *like a tomb.*

They quickly discovered that Reynolds used the single-storey building for storing his toys. Snowboards and mountain bikes hung on metal stanchions, displayed like trophies rather than everyday items. A jet-ski sat on a low-loader behind the garage doors, and there were ropes and climbing equipment hanging on wooden pegs along one wall.

'Liked his outdoor sports,' Wilkins observed.

'Did you know Reynolds?'

'Not to speak to, no. But we've had complaints from the locals about him and his city friends. They tend to party quite hard in the summer.'

She followed him into the lighthouse. The interior had been completely renovated, turned into an open-plan apartment that wouldn't have looked out-of-place in a New York loft. From the notes, she learned that the lighthouse was over seventy feet high, with four-storeys of high-ceilinged rooms. There was a spiral staircase running around the inside of the wall which had been carefully restored to show off the original brickwork.

'Did this guy win the lottery?' Biggs said to himself, taking photographs of the sound system.

'Is it a good one?' Marshall asked.

'Er yeah. Twenty-grand at least.'

Wilkins was breathless by the time they made it to the second floor, which was the kitchen. He made an excuse about needing water and left them to it.

Marshall went up to the next storey leaving Biggs to search the cupboards and praise the man's choice of Le Creuset pans.

She walked into a man cave. There was a large screen monitor suspended from the ceiling and shelves filled with DVDs and games. Reynolds obviously had a penchant for Sci-Fi and Japanese animé; there were rows of graphic novels and plastic figures lined up along one wall. Some still in their original packaging.

Boys and their toys. She thought. *Very expensive toys.*

The third floor doubled up as his office. A glass-topped desk sat in front of a tall window with a stunning view out over the sea. A cluster of six monitors were suspended from an adjustable frame hanging over the desk where a sleek black keyboard and mouse lay slowly glowing.

Beneath the desk, a small server cabinet hummed. Small green lights flickering like Christmas decorations.

'Biggs,' she shouted down the stairs. 'We've got an active server. Tell Frazer to get his team down here pronto.'

She didn't even bother asking whether Wilkins's team had any technical support.

31

ENCRYPTED

London. Friday, December 6. 17:00

The rush hour traffic meant that it was close to five o'clock before they were back into central London. The journey had been slow but Marshall didn't mind, she needed time to think, to process the details of Derek Reynolds's life.

He lived alone in a bachelor's wet dream of a house. One that Biggs would have given his left testicle to borrow for a weekend. Not bad for a boy who'd grown up in social services. There was no evidence of a girlfriend, boyfriend or any significant other. There was a collection of stuff, expensive stuff — *escapism*, was the word that sprung to mind. Reynolds filled his days with adventures either real or virtual. There was very little of 'him' about the place, it was like a photo shoot from a twenty-something lads' mag.

Something was niggling away in the back of her mind. A small annoying thought that wouldn't surface, like a wasp trapped under a glass.

Derek was Head of IT at Credit Suisse, Melanie was in Risk at Lloyd's. Both worked in the city, both had very well paid jobs in the finance sector. Not the kind of work that leads people to want to torture and kill them. She was missing something, these weren't random, too much thought and planning had gone into their execution. The killer had a reason for ending their lives, she just couldn't see what it was.

As they crawled along Moorgate, she stared out at the Christmas lights. It gave the city a fairytale quality, reminding her how much she loved London at this time of year, apart from the drunks and the shoplifting of course.

Marshall's phone buzzed. It was a call from Frazer. She put it on speaker.

'Bad news. The server's drives are all encrypted,' his voice came out over the car speakers. 'Government grade top-secret shit, AES256 or Twofish. Not a chance of cracking it without the password.'

'Told you, he's a hacker. It'll be locked down tighter than Salazar's knickers,' Biggs said.

Marshall glared at him to be quiet. 'Okay. Can you find out who his ISP is and make a request to pull his activity? There might be something useful in there,' she suggested.

Frazer scoffed. 'Yeah, which porn sites he was visiting.'

'He's a bloke, living on his own, what else would he be doing on the internet?' Biggs agreed.

'That's exactly what I was hoping to find out,' Marshall added, interrupting their banter.

The traffic came to a dead stop and Biggs put the car into neutral. Frazer continued. 'If he's in network security, he will know how to hide the dodgy shit: VPNs, proxies, Tor browsers, there are a whole host of tools to mask his activities. This guy has better kit than I do.'

Marshall raised her eyebrows at Biggs.

'He's a geek with expensive toys. From what we saw in his house he was definitely spending above his pay grade. So I think dodgy shit is very likely.'

'Drugs?' Biggs said, putting the car into gear and pulling away slowly.

'What else pays that well?'

'Bitcoin,' said Frazer, 'the guy's got enough computer power in that server rack to mine a decent stack of crypto.'

Marshall had always wanted to ask Frazer about bitcoin, but now was not the time. 'Okay. Thanks. Let me know if you find anything useful.'

She ended the call.

'Bollocks,' she said, staring out of the window.

It felt good to be back in the city, surrounded by the familiar sights. The countryside disturbed her, something about all that space and lack of structure made her feel uneasy. London was like a giant machine, powered by people. It had a rhythm to it, the rush hours were like a heartbeat. She watched them all flowing along the street, making their way towards the tube station in the pouring rain. Five million people worked in London; half a million of them in the city. The average commute was just under an hour. By seven this evening most of them would be safe at home in the suburbs. Except for the eight thousand residents that is, who mostly lived in and around the Barbican. Those guys could be home in minutes. It would have taken Reynolds more like two hours to get back to the lighthouse, but it would have been worth it for that view.

A thought struck her, the thing that had been bugging her finally surfacing.

'Where's his other car?'

'Other car?'

'How did he get to the station that morning? The man obviously likes his cars. Check with the train station CCTV and see what he left in the car park.'

32

STROKE

Island Gardens, Docklands. Friday, December 6. 21:30

When Marshall got home there were two messages from her mother and one from James. She ignored them both and went for a shower.

'I got your email.' James's voice sounded strained and tired. She used to call it his 'Boozehound' voice; deep and gravelly, as if he had smoked too many cigarettes. It used to be quite a turn-on back in the early days when their shifts happened to align and they had nowhere in particular to be on a Saturday morning.

'What's the matter with you Pip?' his message continued, 'You couldn't be arsed to ring me. If you want something at least have the decency to call up and ask. You know I'd always try and help you.'

She listened to the message twice, trying not to imagine

him sitting in some office in Manchester surrounded by gorgeous twenty-three-year-old brunettes.

He was right, of course. Emailing him Devlin's notes had been the coward's way. She would have to face the fact that they needed to talk, but she didn't want to do it without a drink.

The fridge was empty and the recycling bin was full of wine bottles. Not a great start to a Friday night. She couldn't bring herself to have Thai food for a third night running. She was just about to get changed out of her pyjamas and go down to the corner shop, when she remembered the posh pizza place at the end of her road delivered. Opening her laptop, she ordered three bottles of Pinot and a La Reine.

The first message from her mother was short. 'Your father's had a stroke. He's been taken into hospital.'

The second was just a plea to come as soon as possible. It sounded like she had been crying.

Marshall called her back, but it went straight to voicemail. Her mother would regularly turn her mobile phone off to 'save the battery'.

'Fuck!' Marshall screamed at the mirror as she got changed.

She forgot to cancel the pizza.

It was after eleven by the time she got to West Middlesex Hospital. Walking into A&E, she realised it was Friday night and the drunks had already surfaced. Pools of vomit were being mopped up by unimpressed cleaning staff while a loud group of angry men clustered around the main desk complaining about the wait times at the top of their voices.

Marshall flashed her badge at one of the flustered receptionists and was told that her father had been taken to the stroke ward on the third floor.

The last time she visited this hospital was to discuss her father's prognosis. It had been one of the hardest days of her life.

In the space of that thirty-minute consultation she became the head of the family. Her father's regression meant he was no longer legally capable and her mother, always the sensible one, suddenly had no idea what to do. The specialist tried to explain that there were still options, ways to slow the inevitable, new drugs and techniques to hold back the degradation. But when it came down to it, he was telling them that it was only a matter of months not years.

And now that day had come.

She took the stairs to the third floor and found her mother sitting beside his bed, holding his hand.

He gave her a lopsided smile as she walked into the ward, one side of his mouth not quite in sync with the other.

'Hello dear,' he said, with a slight lisp. 'Nice to see you.'

There was that smile in his eyes, the one that meant he recognised her.

Her mother was pale, her eyes reddened and puffy. She gripped his hand tightly, her knuckles whitening.

'It's all right, Mum,' Marshall said, taking a chair from an empty bed and sitting down next to her. 'Just tell me what happened?'

'Sorry to hear about your dad,' James said.

Marshall was sitting on a bench outside the hospital. It was morning and she hadn't really slept. She wasn't sure why she called him, she couldn't think of anyone else to talk to.

'He's okay, for now. But he could have another one, they say the next few weeks are critical.'

'How's your mum?'

She sighed. 'Doing her best. Trying hard to hold on to him for as long as she can.'

'Do you want me to come down?'

'No. I can handle it. I just needed … I don't know. To tell you. I guess.'

'Yeah. Thanks. It's good to hear your voice.'

She bit her lip. Feeling the tears welling in her eyes. There was nothing she wanted more than to have him hold her right now.

'I'm sorry about the email,' she said, changing the subject.

'No problem. I've already started some traces. Should have something for you by Monday. Are you sure you're okay?'

'Thanks, I'm fine. He's no idea what's going on. It's a blessing really. God I sound like my mum.' She laughed.

'Pip, we need to talk. About the baby.'

'Not now for fuck's sake!'

'There's never a right time.'

This was how the argument always began. They were trapped in some kind of loop, neither able to get past this cycle of blame.

'What do you want me to say?' she asked, anger edging her voice. 'I wish it never happened. I wish we were happy. I was the one that lost it, not you. You just sat there and tried not to blame me, and I hated it. You had every right to get angry, but you never did. We aren't designed to deal with that kind of pain. This is not something you can fix, it's just life, we have to move on.'

She ended the call before he had time to respond.

As if the universe was listening, a couple walked out of the hospital proudly carrying their new born baby and she hugged herself, letting the tears come.

33

PULLMAN

The Shard, London Bridge. Friday, December 6. 23:05

T*he city of light*, he thinks to himself looking down over London. The winter night has closed in and the views across the Thames are breathtaking. Millions of tiny points of light glitter across the horizon like souls awaiting judgement in purgatory.

Neither heaven nor hell.

Standing at a thousand feet, The Shard towers over the city. He feels like a god watching the tiny people in the streets below.

In the restaurant seventy floors below, she will be sitting at a table with a group of her friends. Laughing and joking, sipping cocktails, acting as if she were the life and soul of the party. But he knows her smile is nothing more than a mask, a well practised disguise that she has worn so often that she has forgotten who lies beneath it.

I will remind you, he thinks, getting into the lift.

. . .

Samantha Pullman rises from the table, excuses herself and makes her way towards the toilets.

It is Friday night and the restaurant is packed. The overworked staff are rushing from table to table, too busy to notice him follow her into the ladies toilets. Wearing the overalls of the building's service company is like donning a cloak of invisibility, no one pays any attention to the cleaning staff.

The rubber compound in the soles of his boots makes no sound as he checks the stalls. They are all empty except for hers. Hanging the cleaning sign on the door handle, he softly closes the door and locks it.

Under the low fifty-hertz hum of the neon lights he can hear her snorting the white powder.

Cocaine — benzoyl-methyl-ecgonine. Freud's magical substance. How you crave to leave this reality behind.

34

SATURDAY

Chiswick. Saturday, December 7. 14:00

Marshall had taken her mother back home. The house seemed strangely uncomfortable without her dad, like someone had broken in and moved the furniture around while they were out. They were both too exhausted to talk and managed to sleep through most of Saturday morning.

Waking in the afternoon, she went downstairs to find her mother preparing a full English breakfast — one of her father's favourites. Out of habit she had even laid out a third plate at the table.

They ate in silence, neither able to think of anything to say, staring at the empty chair.

Her mother pushed her food around the plate, hardly eating anything.

Her parents moved to Chiswick a few years after Will died. They always insisted it was to be closer to her, but

Marshall knew there were too many memories in Bath, too many people who blamed their daughter for what happened. Her father was offered a position at the Royal College of Architecture and for a while they managed to find some peace. Her mother stayed at home. Part of her seemed to have been left behind in the old house. She made the best of the situation, as she always did, but there was something broken behind her eyes. She hid it well for years, but now it was all too apparent.

The phone rang, its shrill chime shocking them out of their daze. Her mother leapt to her feet and answered it before the third ring.

'Yes,' she said in her phone voice. 'This is Mrs Marshall.'

Bad news. Marshall thought, her heart beating a little faster.

'Oh I see, yes. Thank you.'

She replaced the receiver and went into the kitchen.

Marshall heard the familiar sound of the kettle being filled. 'Was that the hospital?' she asked, coming out with the plates.

Her mother nodded, staring out of the window into the garden, avoiding direct eye contact.

'They're going to keep him in for more tests. Just in case. We can go and visit him later.'

'Best place for him Mum,' Marshall put her hand on her shoulder.

'Yes.'

'Did they tell you which ward?'

Her mother's shoulders shuddered and Marshall could hear the soft sobbing.

She put her arms around her and they cried together.

35

DIPLOMATIC PROTECTION

Wood Street Police Station, London. Sunday, December 8. 08:00

Salazar called an emergency meeting on Sunday morning. The whole squad showed up, they all knew better than to disobey her. *No one dared.*

Marshall was one of the last to arrive. The text from Baxter had come as something of a blessing, an excuse to leave the stifling silence of the hospital room. She didn't want her last memories of her father to be that weak old man lying in a sick bed. She needed to focus on something else. James used to accuse her of "going into her shell", like a crab, but it was just her way of dealing with it. She went back to her flat, put on a suit and focused on the only thing that made any sense — her job.

The DI stood in the middle of the office, her arms folded across her chest like an angry parent, her face impassive and unreadable. On the journey back from the lighthouse, Biggs had passed the time speculating on what Salazar did when she was off duty. He had an active imagination, and the one that stuck with Marshall was the dominatrix at a BDSM party. Marshall still couldn't get the image of Salazar dressed in skintight studded leather out of her head.

'We have a potential third victim,' Salazar began, uncrossing her arms and tapping on a picture of a blonde woman on the plasma screen. The name underneath it read: 'Samantha Pullman.'

'Samantha was last seen on Friday night at the Oblix restaurant in The Shard. Her guests say she went to the toilet at around eleven o'clock and never returned.'

I know her, Marshall thought. The lack of sleep was making it hard to concentrate. She could feel her heart racing, her blood was more caffeinated than the coffee she was holding so the recognition took longer than normal. Her thinking was fuzzy, blurred at the crucial edges of instinct.

Random press photos from parties sprang into her mind. She was famous. No, she was infamous, a spoilt little rich kid who was always in the news for her outrageous behaviour and rockstar lifestyle. It came to her then, the history of drink and drugs. Samantha was the only daughter of one of the most influential men in England; Lord Pullman was reported to have paid off a slew of boyfriends and journalists to keep her reputation intact.

In his usual brusque way, Devlin voiced what everyone else was thinking. 'What's this got to do with our case?'

Salazar smiled, or at least she tried to, it came off as more of a scowl. 'A member of staff found this in the ladies bathroom when they were closing.'

She tapped on the TV screen and a shaky video, obviously shot on someone's phone, showed the inside of a stall, the toilet was stained with blood some of which had been used to draw a single circular symbol on the wall.

Salt, thought Marshall. *Just as the professor described.*

Salazar stopped the video, pausing it on the archaic graffiti.

'There is a chance she may still be alive.'

Doubtful.

'Since this is a potential kidnap situation involving the daughter of a Member of the House of Lords, Protection Command will be getting involved.'

There was a collective groan from the room.

'Look, I know we'd all rather not have PDP riding shotgun, but this is the daughter of a peer of the realm which means we're all going to be under scrutiny.'

She turned her attention to Marshall. 'Which means doing everything by the book.'

The commander of Parliamentary and Diplomatic Protection was a hard-eyed man with close cropped hair. He walked through the office with the air of someone who could kill you with one hand. The two officers following behind him were both armed. Everyone stopped what they were doing to watch them pass, they made no attempt to engage with the specialists, who looked more like soldiers than coppers.

'Cavalry's arrived,' quipped Devlin once they had disappeared into Donovan's office.

'Shit's going to hit the fan when they find out what we've got on the other two,' Biggs added.

'They won't care about the others,' Marshall said, without looking up from the SOCO report on The Shard. 'Their brief will be to find her alive.'

'He's not following his usual MO,' Biggs said.

Marshall pulled out one of the photographs and held it up. 'Have we got the CCTV from The Shard? There's no way he got out of there without getting caught on camera.'

'They're already on it,' Biggs said nodding to the three men in Donovan's office. 'PDP pulled rank.'

The conversation through the glass partition did not look like it was going well. Salazar and Donovan were taking Commander Ford through the investigation and by the expressions on their faces he was asking some tricky questions.

'Have you checked to see if she had any connections to the other victims?'

'She's a spoilt rich brat who spent all her daddy's money getting high. I'm struggling to see how there would be.'

'But maybe it's about the money,' Marshall pondered, picking up Gladwell's financial report. 'Someone paid Melanie a ton of cash for something and no one seems to be able to trace it. Reynolds was living like a millionaire playboy. Where are we at with getting access to his bank account?'

Biggs shrugged, his shirt collar moving to reveal the edges of a love bite on his neck. 'Nothing. Credit Suisse aren't playing ball.'

'He's got a Swiss bank account?'

'Perk of the job I guess. They're citing all kinds of bank treaty and privacy shit.'

'Arrange a meeting with his boss. I think they need to understand how serious this is.'

Donovan opened the door, his face still slightly flushed

from their discussions. He looked like a broken man. The commander followed him out.

'DS Marshall,' he said, waving her over. 'This is Commander Ford. Since you have worked on both the previous victims, we've agreed that you will act as liaison between the two teams.'

Devlin looked pissed off, and Marshall could see the anger burning in Salazar's eyes from the other side of the room. Donovan was giving her the break he promised, but the DI was obviously seething. She nodded to Ford, who reciprocated. It was clear from his expression that he had been forced to take her on.

'Let's make a start on the CCTV shall we?' he said in a well-spoken, Sandhurst accent.

Marshall wished she could have taken a photograph of Salazar's face as she left.

36

THE CLEANER

Wood Street Police Station, London. Sunday, December 8. 10:00

The upper floor of Wood Street was an unusual feature of the Italian design the architects created when they planned the building. The wooden floored ballroom, originally meant for functions, presentations and awards ceremonies had been taken over by the PDP tech team. They were busy unpacking their equipment while Frazer hovered around trying to help get them connected to the network. They moved like soldiers, efficient and professional, there was no banter and no larking around. A bank of six monitors had been set up along one wall.

'You're here as an observer,' Ford said in a tone that was obviously meant as an order. 'Seen but not heard. Are we clear?'

'Yes, sir.' Marshall replied automatically. The caffeine rush now replaced with an adrenaline one, she felt wide awake.

'Have you processed the CCTV Palmer?'

'Just bringing it up now, sir,' Palmer replied, tapping his keyboard. The CCTV footage from The Shard flickered onto each of the screens.

'Subject appears to be dining with guests at twenty-two forty-five,' Palmer noted, zooming up one of the feeds across all six monitors.

Samantha was a beautiful, vivacious woman with curly blonde hair and a red dress that accentuated all of her curves. She reminded Marshall of one of those old-fashioned movie stars, like Marilyn Monroe, the cameras loved her from every flattering angle. She was sitting at a round table by the windows with three men and two women, acting as if she owned the place. *The best seats in the house of course*, Marshall thought, watching her subtly flirting with the man to her right. He was slightly older, maybe mid-forties, and was pouring her another glass of champagne from an expensive-looking bottle. Marshall had always thought it was over-rated, but Samantha obviously loved it.

'Have we identified the other guests?' Ford asked.

Palmer nodded, opening up a company web page with the biographies of the men.'They're investors. She was entertaining them for a client. Some kind of property deal in West London. The other women are executive escorts.'

Prostitutes.

The video played on until Samantha excused herself and made her way to the toilets.

'No CCTV in the loos.' Palmer switched the monitors back to a multi-screen feed. 'The view is obscured, best I can do is the front desk.' He pointed to one screen where they briefly saw Samantha walk behind the reception desk.

'She never came back?' Ford asked.

'No, sir.'

'Do we have a floor plan?'

Palmer handed Ford a tablet displaying a schematic of the restaurant.

Ford tapped on the square next to the toilets. 'What's that?'

'Service elevator.'

'Can you go back?' Marshall said, still watching the video.

The commander glared at her. Palmer's hand hovered over the controls, waiting for his boss to allow it.

'There was a shadow. Someone else was back there,' she added in way of an explanation.

Ford nodded and Palmer rewound the video.

'Stop! There! Just after that couple arrived.'

A well-dressed young couple walked into shot just as a dark shape appeared against the wall. Palmer zoomed the image, it was part human and part rectangle.

'What's that shape?'

Marshall knew immediately. 'Who gets ignored in these kinds of places?'

Ford looked at her blankly.

'House-keeping.'

They scanned through the footage from the other floors. Above the restaurants on levels thirty-four through to fifty-two was a hotel. The service elevators were in constant use.

After half an hour of sifting through the feeds, they found the man coming out of the service lift pushing a linen trolley. He was wearing a standard grey boiler suit and a cap. The basement was badly lit and he kept his head down, as though he knew where the cameras were.

He disappeared between a car and a van, then got in through the driver's door of the van and pulled away.

'Get the licence on that vehicle,' Ford said, picking up his radio.

'Mobilise units, await location.' Then turning to Palmer who was already accessing the ANPR systems. 'What have you got for me?'

A map of London took over the six screens, a line plotting out from The Shard towards Canary Wharf. 'Vehicle was last seen heading towards Harbour Quay.'

Ford repeated the instructions into his microphone.

He turned back to Marshall. 'Good work, Sergeant.'

37

PURSUIT

London. Sunday, December 8. 11:00

Driving at speed through central London on a Sunday morning was exhilarating. The convoy of black Land Rovers tore through the quiet city streets, ignoring red lights and speed limits as they headed for the Blackwall Basin.

Marshall rode in the back beside two heavily armed officers in full body armour. Her heart was racing, the adrenalin buzz making it hard to focus. They were deadly calm, their eyes distant and cold. Beneath the combat helmet and face mask, she thought she recognised Palmer.

Commander Ford sat in the front, speaking a constant stream of instructions into his radio. There were two other vehicles in front of them and somewhere overhead a chopper was en route.

'Ten minutes to target,' reported the driver.

Ford turned around in his chair. 'DS Marshall, do you want to update your team?'

She nodded, taking out her phone and calling Donovan.

'Guv, we're on our way to Canary Wharf. Ford's team have identified a van used in Pullman's abduction. I'll send Biggs the location. We'll need the whole area cordoned off and SOCO asap.'

Donovan's initial response was a stream of expletives that made her glad she wasn't on speaker. This was followed by the sound of him shouting at Devlin and Biggs to get their 'heads out of their arses.'

'You okay?' he finally asked.

The car screeched around a corner at Tower Hill, the force pushing her up against the window. 'Fine, sir.'

'Don't do anything stupid.'

His tone was fatherly, supposedly warning her to stay out of trouble, but she knew what he actually meant was: 'Don't make me look like a fucking idiot for choosing you instead of Salazar.'

She ended the call. 'They're organising a support team.'

Ford handed her a bullet-proof vest. 'Have you had weapons training?'

'No, sir.' She took off her jacket and strapped on the body armour.

'Then stay in the vehicle until we've cleared the area.' He passed her a small radio and an earpiece.

She wanted to mention that there was no history of the killer using automatic weapons, his methods were more creative and cruel, but Ford had made it abundantly clear that he was not a man to be given advice.

The body armour was heavier than the stab vest she used to wear on the beat. The tightening of the straps over her ribs brought back memories of nights patrolling the streets of South London. In those days, she would never have dreamed of being in this situation: a DS working on a murder squad riding shotgun with men who were more accustomed to protecting the Queen.

They located the van, abandoned on a building site behind Canary Wharf known as Harbour Quay. It was part of the redevelopment of the Blackwall Basin. Between half-finished concrete towers, Marshall spotted narrow boats moored in the small harbour, reminding her of the ones she had seen on her run the week before.

She was thrown violently forward as the car skidded to a halt. Palmer's arm shot out to stop her from smashing her head into the front seat. Marshall turned to thank him, but he was already out of the door.

Moving silently down the bank, she watched the team head for the waste ground. They moved like predatory cats stalking a bird.

Ford was first to the van. With his free hand he signalled his men to surround the vehicle. They spread out in a circle, keeping their weapons trained on the target. It was a VW transporter, the kind of panel van most builders used, the perfect choice if you wanted to blend in with London traffic.

Ford's voice spoke over her headset as he peered into the truck's window.

'No sign of the driver.'

'Roger that,' echoed Palmer, moving towards the rear of the van.

The helicopter hovered overhead. Its rotors chopping the air, stirring the sandy soil into tiny dust tornadoes.

'Anything on thermal?' the commander asked the pilot.

'Affirmative. It's showing a heat source, possibly a body.'

'Any radio frequencies?'

'Negative. Cell towers are offline.'

The windows of the rear doors had been blacked out. Palmer crouched down, taking out a small hand mirror and checking under the van for any sign of explosives.

He gave the thumbs up as Ford joined him.

'Checking the rear doors,' the commander said, swinging his rifle behind his back and taking hold of the handle. He opened the door slightly, looking along the gap for signs of wires or booby traps.

Palmer stepped back a few feet and sighted his gun at the back door, nodding to Ford to proceed.

Marshall didn't like the way this was playing out. From what she had learned about the killer's MO he would never be stupid enough to leave such an obvious piece of evidence. He was meticulous, he never left a trail, and there was always a message in his work.

'Wait!' she barked into the headset, getting out of the car.

It was too late.

Ford pulled on the handle of the door and it swung open.

A fireball blossomed out of the back of the van, and she felt the blast lift her off her feet, slamming her into the side of the Land Rover.

38

HARBOUR QUAY

Harbour Quay, Canary Wharf. Sunday, December 8. 11:45

'Christ, Marshall. Are you ok?' She heard Biggs's voice through a hazy fog.

There was ringing in her ears and it felt like someone had hit her over the head with a lump hammer. She felt hands on her, helping her get to her feet.

'Get off!' she shouted, pushing them away.

'Medic, over here,' shouted Biggs. 'She's still alive.'

Marshall opened her eyes, blinking against the bright sunlight. Biggs's face was looming over her, she had never seen him look so worried.

'Where am —' she began, and then remembered the explosion, all of Ford's team were caught in the blast.

'Ford?'

Biggs shook his head.

He helped her get to her feet and immediately regretted it. A wave of nausea swept over her and she doubled over and threw up.

'Medic!' Biggs screamed at the ambulance.

'I'm all right,' she insisted, wiping her mouth with the back of her hand. There was something sticky on it, she looked down at the blood and felt the world spin away.

When she came around again, she could hear Donovan's dulcet tones somewhere off in the distance. There were ambulances and fire engines blocking her view of the van, but a dark column of smoke wound up from behind them reminding her what she had witnessed.

'How long was I out?'

'We got here fifteen minutes ago. The van went up a few minutes before that. Why didn't he wait for the bomb squad?'

She couldn't remember, the combination of adrenalin, no sleep and too much caffeine had made the whole experience a blur.

The medic arrived and sat Marshall down in the boot of the Land Rover while he did an initial examination.

Once he was happy she wasn't too badly concussed, he gave her a drink. Her mouth was dry, and tasted of ashes and blood. He explained that she had cracked her head against the side of the car, that she was going to need stitches and there was a sizeable swelling on the back of her skull, which hurt like hell when the medic prodded it.

'Did any of them survive?' she asked Biggs, when the medic finished.

Biggs nodded. 'Ford and Palmer took the full force of the blast. The rest were far enough away. They've been taken to St. Thomas's.'

She felt cold and shivered uncontrollably. Marshall knew it was the shock kicking in. Her mind cleared for a moment, allowing her to think more rationally. 'Donovan's going to send me home,' she whispered to Biggs as the DCI appeared from behind an ambulance and walked towards them.

'He has to. You're in shock, and probably concussed.'

'We got close this time. There's going to be something he missed. He rushed this one, something didn't go to plan.'

Biggs looked at her strangely. 'Like he didn't plan to detonate the van?'

'I can't say what exactly. But, this isn't where it was supposed to happen. It's not his style. He likes places connected with history, not building sites.'

'DS Marshall,' Donovan interrupted. 'How's the head?'

'I'm fine, sir.'

'Bollocks. I've spoken to the medic. He's advising a couple of days sick leave. Now don't argue!' he added as she went to protest. 'I should never have agreed to this lunacy. There'll be an internal investigation and I need you at your best. Biggs take a statement from her and then take her home.'

'Yes, Guv.'

39

HOME

Island Gardens, Docklands. Sunday, December 8. 14:00

Biggs recorded Marshall's version of events on his phone while they drove back to her flat. She felt numb recalling the last few hours; recounting the events as if they had happened to someone else. There were still parts that made no sense, so she kept to the facts, leaving out her thoughts on what went wrong. That was for others to decide.

'The helicopter reported a heat source in the back. They thought it might be a body. Ford checked there were no mobile signals and Palmer looked under the van for a bomb. I tried to stop them, but they were too focused on getting to her.'

He helped her into the flat and put the kettle on. Biggs knew her well enough not to ask questions — that was why they got along so well, he let her have her space, the perfect partner in many ways, if he wasn't so damned young.

He left once she had promised to call him later.

She knew the tears would come soon, once the shock wore off.

Her clothes smelled of smoke and blood. She walked into the shower fully dressed and turned it on. Kneeling down, she let the hot water wash away the pain.

Crying in the shower was something she learned to do when Will died. She hid her grief from her parents. They were lovely, caring people but her loss wasn't something that she wanted to share. The only place in the house where she would be left alone was the bathroom and the noise of the shower covered the sound of her sobbing. It was a ritual that continued throughout her adult life.

When they had lost the baby, she would disappear for hours. Telling James that she was shaving her legs or something equally feminine so she could be alone.

Some people could talk endlessly about their problems. Marshall preferred to keep them tightly locked away in a box with all the other painful memories.

The medic had given her some heavy painkillers, she took four and passed out.

Sixteen hours later, she woke to find there were seven text messages from Biggs, two from Donovan and even one from Salazar, which came as something of a shock.

Marshall made herself a strong coffee and drank it sitting on the balcony in her pyjamas. Watching the barges and pleasure cruises chugging their way blithely up and down the Thames. It was comforting to know that people were getting on with their day; going about their life oblivious to the terrible things that she had to deal with. That was the whole point of her job, to make sure that other people didn't have to witness the horrors. *Blissful ignorance,* she thought, feeling the caffeine begin to take effect, *sometimes it would be nice to have a little bit of that. It was why so many of us drink, it helps to shut out the nightmares.*

Her phone rang. It was her mother.

'Your father's better today,' she began, not even asking how Marshall was. 'He's had his breakfast and wants to know when he's going home.'

Marshall bit her lip to stop herself from crying. *He's not going home mum.*

They talked about boring things, like getting him some slippers and how it was so hot in the ward that he was constantly kicking off his covers. It was easier to talk about the little things. Their conversation fell into a pattern, like knitting, sticking to the familiar subjects until they threaded together a sense of normality. One that held back the grim truth — that everything was about to change.

An hour later, Marshall was dressed and her head was beginning to feel less like someone might have used it as a football. She felt ready to face the world once more.

The intercom buzzed. It was Biggs, holding a large bag of Thai food to the camera.

'When did you move in?' he asked, looking around at the cardboard boxes

'A month ago,' she said, tucking into the Pad Thai.

'Are you actually thinking of staying?'

She pulled a face. 'It's complicated.'

'I don't know how you can live like this.'

'There's a system. Kind of. Anyway, tell me about the case. Did they find Pullman?'

He shook his head, stealing the last of the spring rolls with his chopsticks. 'Nope. Her father is pulling all sorts of strings. Wants an official inquiry into the explosion.'

'She wasn't in the van though was she?'

'Forensics have been all over it. There was a simple timer mechanism, hooked up to some volatile chemicals that don't play well with oxygen. That's what the thermal camera picked up, some kind of chemical reaction. They reckon the timer fucked up, and opening the doors caused the thing to blow.'

Marshall scowled, the lines furrowing her brow. 'It wasn't a booby trap. It's not his style.'

'So he has a style now?'

'He was torching the van, erasing the evidence. Something went wrong.'

'Yeah, you said that when I found you.'

'Did I? I don't remember. Fuck I must have been out of it.'

He put down his food. 'You seemed pretty convinced. You said it was to do with history.'

Marshall ran her fingers through her hair, wincing as her fingers found the egg-shaped lump. She closed her eyes, trying to remember exactly what she had said. 'I think it was something the professor said about the Monument. He believes the killer picks his sites carefully, as part of the message he's leaving us. I just knew there was something wrong about where he parked the van. I don't know exactly, it just seemed too random. There was nothing there to give it meaning.'

'Give meaning to what?'

'Her death.'

40

ANJ

Island Gardens, Docklands. Tuesday, December 10. 11:15

The second night, Marshall slept without the aid of sedatives. Her dreams were full of strange, half-remembered things: the first time with Will in the barn behind his house; an argument with her mother about a stray cat she brought home; James taking her away for the weekend to Paris. They left her feeling sad and nostalgic. She decided she needed to spend time with someone who didn't want to talk about work or dementia.

She called Anj.

Anjelina was the kind of old friend with whom you didn't need to stay in regular contact. She was a production director for an ad agency and permanently planning her next trip.

They met at primary school and had been best friends ever since. Following each other through GCSE's and on to college. Anj was always the first one to the bar, offering some story about an ex-boyfriend paying her back when she produced a wad of ten-pound notes.

Marshall found out later that Anj was supplying half of the county with dope, but by then they had all moved on.

'Hello stranger,' her voice sounded muffled, 'hold on love, let me plug these stupid headphones in.'

Marshall waited as instructed.

'Right,' Anj continued, 'how's my favourite detective?'

'Bored. Where are you?' It was always a loaded question with Anj.

'London, flying out to Singapore tomorrow. Filming an ad for Nike. I've got a great pair of trainers that would probably fit you if you're interested. They've sent us a load of freebies.'

'No, I'm good,' Marshall replied, her calves still aching from the last run. 'Listen. Do you want to meet up before you go? I know it's short notice, but I could really do with an Anj special.'

'Hold on.' There was a short pause and Marshall could hear rapid tapping on a keyboard.

'Okay, just cancelled my meetings. Where do you want to start? I can get an Uber over to yours and pick you up?'

'No, I've moved. I'll meet you in Charlotte Street.'

'Oh, we're going to start fancy are we?' Anj said in a mocking posh voice. 'Was a time when we would've been happy with a pint of snakebite in the Marquee.'

'I didn't say we were going to stay there.'

'Fair enough, petal. See you in an hour.'

Just talking to Anj was like snorting a line of cocaine, which used to be another of her friend's vices. There weren't many problems that couldn't get sorted during an afternoon session with her.

Before she left the flat, Marshall checked in with her mother, there was still no change. She decided it was better not to mention that she was on sick leave or that the rest of the day was going to be spent in the company of Anj. Her mother had always taken a dim view of her best friend. In her eyes she was the kind of girl that got one into all sorts of trouble, especially with boys.

Which is exactly what Marshall needed right now.

41

CONFESSIONS

Charlotte Street Hotel, London. Tuesday, December 10. 13:00

Marshall realised she hadn't seen her friend in nearly a year, but ten minutes later it felt more like a couple of weeks. They had lunch in the Charlotte Street Hotel spending the first hour chatting about the old days. It was a ritual with them, reminiscing over the times when life was less complicated and far more exciting, always helped to kick the session off on the right foot — especially when Anj had some juicy gossip about the people they used to hang around with.

'So, remember Paula Fenwick? The one whose chest appeared in year ten,' she said, pushing her breasts up and pouting.

Marshall snorted, something only Anj could make her do. 'Yeah, she stole my boyfriend.'

Anj waved her hand as if it meant nothing. 'She shagged everyone's boyfriend. Anyway, turns out she was caught giving one of her kid's teachers a blow job.' Poking her tongue into the side of her cheek so it bulged.

Marshall nearly spat out her wine. 'What?'

'Parents' evening is never going to be the same again.'

The waiter arrived with the food, catching the end of the conversation. He was young with dark eyes and Anj had already flirted with him when they arrived. Marshall loved how confident she was with men, they were like toys to her, which was probably why she had never stayed with one for any length of time.

After they drained the first bottle and caught up on the gossip, things grew more serious. Anj listened attentively while Marshall told her about James and the baby. It was always easy to talk to her, the words just came flowing out. When she went on to tell her about her father's dementia it was harder, perhaps because her dad always had a soft spot for her. The 'happy-go-lucky-girl' he used to call Anj, and she was, most of the time. There were tears, but that was okay.

They talked about the case too. Her friend never questioned why Marshall had joined the force after Will died. It was an unspoken thing between them, until she moved into CID, then Anj would plead with her to hear about the gruesome details of her latest investigation. It wasn't strictly professional, but if there was one person she trusted above all others, it was Anj.

She told her about Melanie and Reynolds, about the strange symbols and the way the killer had taken her tongue and his eyes. When she got to the explosion at Harbour Quay Anj's eyes went wide.

'You nearly died?'

'It's not the first time.'

Her friend grabbed her hand. 'This is serious, I can't

bear the thought of a world without you in it.' There were tears welling in her eyes. 'You're the sensible one remember? Who knows what would happen to me if I didn't have you to keep me grounded.'

Marshall squeezed her hand. 'I promise not to die.'

Anj wiped her eyes. 'Okay so, tell me more about this professor,' She poured them both a large glass of wine and upended the empty bottle into the ice bucket just as the waiter returned with the dessert menu.

'Nothing to tell really. He's an academic, teaches medieval history at King's.'

Her friend scoffed. 'I didn't ask for his CV. What does he look like?'

'He's a bit like the bloke off that movie.'

'Going to need a bit more than that honey. Are we talking Robert De Niro or Patrick Swayze?'

Marshall clicked her fingers. 'No, you know, the one with the dinosaurs.'

'Jurassic Park?'

'Yes. The brainy one.'

Anj's eyes widened. 'Jeff Goldblum,' she said with an air of approval. 'Nice work. I do like an older man with a twinkle.'

'I didn't say he had a twinkle.'

But there was something about him. She hadn't realised until Anj brought it up. He was older, but not that old, and self-assured to the point of arrogance.

'And you say he turned up out of the blue the other day?'

Marshall nodded. 'My boss thinks he's stalking me.'

'Well, that settles it. He's either your serial killer or he wants to get in your knickers. Or both.' Anj raised one eyebrow and giggled to herself.

'Did you ever meet Samantha Pullman?' Marshall asked,

suddenly remembering that Anj used to go to the same kind of parties.

Anj closed her eyes for a second. 'Blonde, rich — daddy was something in the Government?'

'Yes, and he still is.'

'Once or twice. While I was dating that twat with the hedge fund. God he was a boring fucker — literally.'

Marshall could feel the wine loosening her tongue. She leaned in and whispered. 'She's gone missing.'

Her friend didn't seem concerned. 'I'm surprised she's survived this long. She used to hang out with some real seedy arseholes: Russian mafia and worse. If ever there was someone begging to be kidnapped it was Sam Pullman.' She picked up the menu. 'Now, enough talk about work and let's sort out the dessert.'

42

RIVER POLICE

River Thames. Wednesday, December 11. 06:30

The river is high and flowing fast after a week of torrential rain.

A police launch bobs up and down in the strong tidal flow, its skipper gunning the twin engines, doing his best to keep them stationary while the divers haul the body into the back of the boat.

Trains clatter overhead, the first of the commuters crossing over the bridge into Cannon Street.

'This is Romeo-Oscar-five, recovery of a female, IC-1, mid-thirties,' the captain says into the radio, watching his crew place their find into a body bag. 'Identification unlikely. Over.'

The head and face of the woman has suffered terrible mutilation. The skipper has worked the river for twenty-five years, he's seen what a boat propeller can do to a body.

'Copy Romeo-Oscar. Central want to know if it's Pullman? Over,' the operator's voice comes through the speaker.

'No idea. Returning to base. Over,' replies the captain, turning the wheel towards Wapping.

The divers rip off their masks and take out respirators as the boat accelerates away. The younger of the two stares blankly at the damage, like a fascinated child seeing something for the first time. It reminds the skipper of the first one he ever saw, half-eaten and bloated, there was no easy way to prepare someone for their first corpse.

The river was a harsh mistress when she wanted to be.

43

SHARD

The Shard, London Bridge. Wednesday, December 11. 10:00

Marshall had never been a great one for heights. The official term for it was vertigo, but for her it was just pure fear.

Donovan called to tell her about the body they pulled from the river, but she already knew; Biggs had texted her an hour before and she was on her way to The Shard when the DCI rang.

The restaurant was on the thirty-fourth floor, and the ride up in the lift was remarkably quick. She kept her eyes shut, holding her breath until the doors opened.

The manager was waiting for her when she stepped out. He was a thin, anxious-looking man with dark shadows under his eyes. His restaurant had been closed since the incident on Friday and she could see he was having sleepless nights over the losses he was taking.

At least he'll be cooperative, she thought. *The sooner we're finished the sooner he can open.*

'Detective?' He asked with an unsure inflection. She often got mistaken for someone younger, she just had good genes.

'DS Marshall,' she confirmed, showing him her warrant card.

He relaxed a little. 'Would you like a drink?'

Marshall thought about the night before and shook her head. Anj had dragged her into the Groucho Club on Dean Street after they finally finished lunch and then it had got really messy. It was full of actors, musicians and their agents, all of whom Anj seemed to know in some random way. Marshall had been sensible and switched to drinking water, but Anj's new friends insisted on rounds of shots. How the hell Anj managed to get on a 6am flight to Singapore was beyond her.

'The toilets?' Marshall asked the manager, looking around the empty bar.

With the grace of a man who had spent his entire life in the service industry, he bowed and motioned her to follow him. 'This way please.'

The ladies toilet was still taped off. Forensics had swept the place, but they wouldn't release it until the physical evidence had been processed. The manager stopped at the door as Marshall stepped into the empty room.

The strip lights in the ceiling sensed her presence and flickered to life. She caught a reflection of herself in the long mirror by the washbasins and grimaced. In the rush to get out of the flat this morning she'd hardly had time to put a brush through her hair. Taking out a band, she pulled her hair back into a tight pony tail.

Pushing open the door of the stall, the words of the report came back to her.

Traces of cocaine found on the lid of the cistern. Victim's fingerprints were present on the door handle and the walls.

Blood was smeared on the white porcelain bowl and the marble tiles of the floor. There were footprints and other marks of a struggle captured in the pool that spread around the base of the toilet.

Her eyes were drawn to the symbol on the wall above the cistern. Painted in blood was a circle with a horizontal line running through its centre. *Salt*, she thought, pulling out her phone and taking a photograph. *Gresham was right.*

Marshall closed her eyes, trying to imagine how he would have attacked her. The blood was most likely from a head wound. Had she slipped and cracked her skull in the fight? From what Anj had told her, Samantha Pullman was no push over. Perhaps that was what had changed the pattern, she fought back before he could tranquillise her.

Gates had found traces of GHB in the first two victims, so the killer would have had to get near enough to inject her. This wasn't like a crowded street during rush hour, where the crush of bodies would make it easy to get up close to someone. Samantha had also been using drugs since she was a teenager, so maybe she could tolerate a higher dose than normal people.

Why here and not in the city like the others? She asked herself. If it wasn't for the symbol, Marshall would have said this was a different person. The Met only contacted Donovan because of the graffiti. No one wanted the expense of a serial case, they were only too happy to hand it over.

Marshall looked down at the footprints, the report said they were a size eleven boot. Their first piece of physical evidence. The man was at least six-foot tall. Biggs was working with the CCTV footage to get a better physical description, but it was hard, the killer had done his homework, he knew the viewing angle of every one of the cameras. Not one of them got a shot of his face.

Why didn't he just shut the CCTV down like he did at Monument? Marshall wondered. *Perhaps he's getting braver, more daring.*

It was good to finally have some idea of what he looked like. Before this, he was a phantom; a ghost formed from the shadows of his actions. Marshall usually pictured them as faceless beings when she surveyed a crime scene, visualising the murder. Now at least she knew the shape of him, even if it was nothing more than an outline. It helped to see him as something other than just a murderer — creating a three dimensional profile, thinking of him as a man with a life, a family, even friends. One that walked his dog, bought groceries and paid his taxes. And yet somewhere within all of that normality was the thing that drove him to murder, that unlocked the strictures of normal social behaviour and made him take that step into the dark.

Most murders were committed by people who knew the victim: a jilted lover, a jealous boyfriend — they were emotional crimes. Others were motivated by greed or the result of mental health issues, but the number of serial killings in the UK in the last three years could be counted on the fingers of one hand.

If this was his third victim, then the case would be classified as a serial killing and that meant a whole circus of other departments getting involved.

It was also the kind of case that could get you promoted. She could see Salazar rubbing her hands together at the idea of it turning into something bigger. The woman was nothing if not ambitious.

. . .

When Marshall came out of the toilets the manager was looking at his mobile phone.

'They've found her,' he said, holding it up so she could see the news story.

The headline read: 'Heiress found in the Thames.' There was a grainy video of a police launch and divers hauling a body bag into the boat.

Bollocks, thought Marshall.

44

PROFESSOR

King's College. Wednesday, December 11. 12:00

Marshall left The Shard and made her way towards King's College. She could have taken the tube, but she wanted time to think and she needed to get some air.

Crossing London Bridge, a bitterly cold east wind suddenly rose up from the river. She stopped and turned towards it, breathing in the cold air. It tasted clean and sharp, numbing her face and making her lungs ache. It reminded her of the skiing trip the school had organised to Switzerland. She was fifteen and twenty hours on a coach had been worth it just for the views of the mountains. *I need a holiday*, she promised herself, *as soon as this case is over.*

The wind dropped and a shaft of sunlight broke through the clouds, lighting up the glittering glass towers of Canary Wharf. Beneath her feet, the bow of a barge appeared from under the bridge. The open hold was filled to the brim with rubbish and the smell wafted up to greet her. She buried her face into her scarf to stop herself from gagging. *This was the real London*, she thought, *a city of two halves.*

She watched the waves ripple out along the thin, garbage-strewn banks, washing plastic bottles further up the muddy sides, and wondered how many corpses had been pulled out of the Thames.

Donovan told her that the body had been found between Charing Cross and Westminster Bridge. Since the river was tidal, it meant that the killer could have dumped her into the water at Harbour Quay and the body drifted down with the flow. They had yet to make a positive ID, he said that her face had been too mutilated to be sure — they were waiting on DNA.

King's College was a beautiful building: the grey stone portico with its regency columns reminded Marshall of a museum. Her father had always wanted her to go to university, and she would have done if it hadn't been for Will. She received unconditional places at Cambridge and Edinburgh the week before he died. She could still see the look of pride on her father's face when he read the letters and later, the pain when she told him she wouldn't accept them.

The professor's study was a minimalist space with sleek black leather sofas and a glass desk. It looked more like a therapist's consulting room than the antiquated book-lined study that she was expecting.

'Please sit down,' Gresham said, motioning to one of the chairs. 'Can I get you some tea?'

'No, thank you,' she said, finding the sofa more comfortable than she thought it would be. Everything about him had an air of quality. He was wearing his usual black polo neck under a tweed jacket, and a pair of dark jeans.

Marshall smiled inwardly, remembering the conversation with Anj. He definitely had a twinkle, it was the intense way he looked at her, as if he was staring into her soul.

Gresham sat on the opposite couch. 'Have you something else for me?' he asked, folding his arms.

No small talk, she liked that. She took out her phone and showed him the image of the symbol from the stall.

'Ah, may I?' he said, taking the phone.

He took off his glasses and studied the picture, narrowing his eyes.

Too vain to admit he needs reading glasses? She noted.

'Salt, as I predicted.'

'How did you know?'

'Paracelsus added salt to Aristotle's first two elements. It represents the body. Whoever killed these people is marking them with the *Tria Prima*. The three primes. Where was she found?' he asked without looking up.

'In the river,' she replied.

He frowned and shook his head. 'No, not in water, that's a completely separate element.'

The professor handed back the phone and took out his notebook, drawing the symbols on a blank page. 'So far he's used the cypher for air and fire, two of the four Hermetic elements. Water would make a third, but that—' He pointed at her phone. 'Is salt — it wouldn't make sense to put her in water.'

'The Thames is tidal where they found the body, it would be sea water.'

He didn't appear to be convinced.

'What's Hermetic?' she asked.

'It's a classical tradition that proposed that everything in nature was comprised from four base elements: earth, fire, wind and water or variants of such. The Persians had a fifth known as "void" and the Chinese introduced metal into the mix, but essentially it was the same. They all tried to reduce the universe into its base elements.'

'Like the periodic table.'

He nodded, his expression softening. Marshall felt like a student who had just given the right answer in a test.

'I hardly think you could compare it to Mendeleev's table, but it does align with the alchemical principle of *prima materia*, which states that everything can be broken down into its component parts.'

'So why do you think she ended up in the water?'

He shrugged. 'Unless I'm very much mistaken, whoever you pulled from the river is not your killer's latest victim.'

Marshall was confused. 'How can you be sure?'

'Because there is method in his madness,' he quoted. 'Alchemists were experimental scientists. Your killer is testing his art, perfecting it if you will. He is creating his Magnum Opus.'

'And what exactly is that?'

Gresham drew another group of symbols, a circle within a square surrounded by a triangle.

'The great work. A personal transformation towards immortality. It's a process that leads to the creation of the philosopher's stone. There are four stages, usually represented by colours or alchemical symbols like the swan, raven or phoenix. Your murderer is on a spiritual journey.'

'To where?'

The professor held up his hands. 'Personal enlightenment?'

'People don't kill to find their inner self.'

He shrugged. 'Manson convinced his followers of something similar.'

'You've studied Manson?' It was her turn to be impressed.

'When you've spent long enough studying the medieval, you realise that we're not so different to our ancestors. There are patterns of human behaviour that repeat throughout history. We haven't progressed as much as we think. People are still driven by the same motives.'

'Love, hate and money.'

He leaned forwards, his eyes burning brightly. 'And sex.'

She felt a flush of heat rising up from her chest into her cheeks.

Trying to ignore the feeling, Marshall continued. 'So what is he going to do next?'

Gresham leaned back in his chair and folded his arms once more. 'I would need access to all of the facts before I could make that kind of prediction. The symbols are only part of his story. The victims will not have been chosen at random, nor the locations.'

Marshall walked out of the college, glad to be back in the cold air. The man was beginning to get under her skin and she didn't like it. Talking to him created more questions than answers, and his insistence that the body in the river wasn't Samantha Pullman was disturbing her most of all.

Her phone rang.

It was Biggs.

45

CREDIT SUISSE

Lower Thames Street. Wednesday, December 11. 15:00

Biggs was waiting outside Credit Suisse. Baxter had finally managed to arrange a meeting with someone from their HR department. In the time it had taken her to get back from King's College, every major news channel had picked up the story of the Thames victim.

'Salazar's going ballistic.'

'Do we know who leaked it?'

Biggs shook his head. 'Probably one of the river squad, although they're denying it.'

'Where did the video come from?'

'Someone on an early morning run, although I'm not sure how the press found out Pullman was missing.'

'I doubt Ford's PDP team were very discreet when they interviewed her dinner guests. It doesn't take a rocket scientist to work out who they were looking for.'

Marshall tried not to take any pleasure from the fact that Salazar would be answering some tough questions from the Superintendent right now.

'Her father is going to be making a statement later,' Biggs added, 'he's going to demand an inquiry.'

'He's going to demand Donovan's head on a silver plate.'

'You are aware that under the provisions of GDPR we cannot disclose information on any of our employees,' said the officious personnel officer.

'This is a criminal investigation,' Marshall reminded her. 'The Data Protection Act has an exception for the purposes for the apprehension of an offender.'

The HR woman's expression softened slightly. 'We will endeavour to assist you in any way we can.'

Marshall sat forward in the chair. 'Derek Reynolds was Head of IT is that correct?'

She nodded. 'Mr Reynolds was a security specialist within our algorithmic trading department.'

'And what does that mean exactly?'

'Our company executes 10 million trades every day, worth approximately six trillion dollars. Reynolds was involved in protecting the systems that process these transactions.'

'And how long has he been with your company?'

The woman looked down at her notes. 'Three years.'

'And before that? Do you have his previous employer?'

'I'm sure you can find that on LinkedIn.'

Marshall felt the anger rising. She had met all types of jobsworths in her time, they all seemed to get some perverted pleasure from making her job harder. She counted backwards from ten and then continued.

'Can you at least tell me if he worked for Lloyd's before joining you?'

The woman smiled. 'We do not hire from our competitors.'

Close enough, thought Marshall.

'Are there any friends or colleagues we could speak to?' Biggs said, changing the subject.

'I didn't know him personally, but by all accounts he was something of a loner. Most of his team were consultants, or offshore teams. There's nothing on his record to suggest he was anything but the most diligent of employees.'

Perhaps at work, Marshall thought, remembering the images that Biggs had grabbed from his Instagram account.

'May I see it?' Biggs asked.

The woman closed the folder and took off her glasses. 'As I said in my email, not without a warrant. His records contain confidential business information.'

'And his bank accounts,' Biggs continued, placing a search warrant on the desk. 'Under the Drug Trafficking Act 1994, you are legally obliged to produce all financial records that relate to Mr Derek Reynolds.'

'Drugs?' exclaimed the woman, picking up the warrant.

Biggs smiled at her. 'We have reason to believe that Derek may have been involved in the supply of Class A drugs.'

46

POST MORTEM

Westminster Mortuary, London. Thursday, December 12. 09:00

Gates was washing the victim when Marshall walked into the lab.

The body was in a terrible state. Its skin mottled in various shades of greyish-green and there were deep lacerations along the torso. Most of the face had been carved off but the back of the skull was still intact, and Marshall could see the blonde hair as he hosed away the last of the river mud.

'Propeller,' explained the pathologist, pointing to the cyclic wounds along her thorax.

'Do you have an idea on how long she's been in the water?'

He took a metal probe out of the rectum and checked the temperature. 'Core body temperature is pretty low. Based on the decay I would say she's been in the river for at least two days, but hard to say for sure. I would need to know how cold the water was to be accurate.'

'Can you tell how she died?'

'Well, that's the odd thing, the water in her lungs isn't from the Thames,' he said, pointing at the two large lobes that sat in a metal tray. 'She was drowned in fresh water and then dumped. The submersion and the boat trauma have eradicated most of the physical evidence. I did find ligature marks on her wrists that indicate she was bound while still alive.'

'Any trace of GHB in her blood?'

Gates shook his head. 'Not yet, I'm still waiting for the results. I can tell you what she had for her last meal.'

Marshall tried to remember what Pullman was eating at the table in the CCTV. 'Oysters?'

'Pasta.'

Marshall walked around the table looking for symbols. 'Did he...'

'Mark her? Oh yes.' He pointed to her hands. 'Both of them.'

The fingers had contracted into claws, the ragged nails caked with dirt. On each palm was carved the same symbol, a downward pointing triangle.

Not salt, she thought, *they didn't match*.

'Something wrong detective?'

'Do you think she could have been in the water longer than two days?'

He shrugged. 'If the temperature of the Thames was low enough, yes.'

Marshall took a picture of the symbol and attached it to an email. She was about to send it to Biggs when she changed her mind and selected the professor instead.

. . .

Walking out of the lab, she took a few deep breaths until the smell of the rotting corpse had cleared, then she called Donovan.

'Guv, I'm at the post-mortem. This isn't Samantha Pullman. I think we've got another, earlier victim.'

47

BOSS

Wood Street Police Station, London. Thursday, December 12. 11:00

Donovan sat with his arms crossed and Salazar leaned on the corner of her desk while Marshall told them about the body. It was clear from both their expressions that neither of them wanted to have this conversation.

'The marks are wrong,' Marshall explained, showing them the photos of the drowned woman's hands. 'Gresham told me that our killer is on some journey of enlightenment. That he has a specific order, a process that he has to follow to achieve his goal.'

Salazar shook her head in disbelief. 'I'm going to need more than some mystic symbols before I go back to Lord Pullman and tell him that it's not his daughter.'

'Okay. Samantha was eating oysters at the restaurant. It's right there on the CCTV. The pathologist's report will say her stomach contents was mostly pasta. If the temperature of the Thames was low enough the body could have been dumped days before Pullman was taken.'

The DI scowled. 'Assuming that was her last meal, who is it then? If it's not Pullman, and where is Samantha if this isn't her?'

Marshall shrugged. 'I don't know. My gut is telling me something went wrong with her murder. Either she's still alive or we haven't found her yet.'

'He's kept her?' It was Donovan's turn to sound surprised. 'That doesn't fit his MO. Why would he do that?'

Before she had a chance to answer Salazar asked: 'Have you been cleared by the doctor for active duty?'

'I haven't had a chance,' Marshall replied sheepishly.

Donovan groaned and Salazar threw up her hands. 'You're not even supposed to be here. Go home and leave this to us.'

'Bollocks,' Marshall swore under her breath. The last thing she wanted now was to get kicked off the case. There were rules about returning to work after an incident and it involved a medical exam. Which was not something she wanted to go through right now.

She took the back stairs out of the office to avoid bumping into the rest of the team, but Biggs caught up to her as she was going through the rear exit.

'Hey, we need to talk.'

'Not here,' Marshall replied. 'At mine, later. Bring a copy of the case reports.'

Biggs nodded. 'No problem, will there be food?'

48

LINES OF ENQUIRY

Island Gardens, Docklands. Thursday, December 12. 18:00

Biggs turned up at her flat with a box full of files and they spent the best part of an hour sticking the crime scene photos onto the blank walls.

'You know, I think it's really added something to the place,' he said when they had covered most of her living room.

'There are beers in the fridge,' Marshall said, kicking off her shoes and sitting on the sofa.

'Are we going to eat?' he asked, opening the fridge. 'Wow. That's real food.'

'Piss off. I do know how to cook. It's just not worth it for one.'

He came back to the living room with a beer and a large glass of white wine. 'Well, I'm honoured.'

She took the glass. 'You know Salazar could have you suspended for bringing me this.'

'Yeah,' he agreed, sitting down beside her. 'But she's too

busy trying to deal with the press to care about what we're doing. Lord Pullman was threatening all sorts of shit.'

'Has she told him about the evidence I found?'

He shook his head. 'No, she's waiting for the DNA results.'

Why should she? I sound like a crazy person.

Marshall changed the subject. 'How did you get on with Reynolds's bank account?'

Biggs dug around in the box of files and pulled out a statement. There were luminous yellow lines through some of the transactions. 'Five years ago Derek got a very healthy payout. Same deal as Melanie, off-shore account for a corporation called Quicksilver Trading. I tried digging around but came up with sweet FA.'

Marshall took the bank statement and studied the numbers. 'Wow, that's a lot more than Melanie!'

She picked up her phone, took a shot of the bank details and sent it on to James.

'Yeah, and it wasn't the only one. He's been receiving annual payouts from other off-shores every year since,' he said, handing her another set of statements with post-it notes marking the relevant pages.

'The man had over ten million in various Swiss accounts when he died.'

'And no one to leave it to?'

'No, I double-checked, there's no sign of any living relative.'

Marshall put down the papers and took a sip of her wine. 'Did you find his car at the station?'

Biggs took out his phone and showed her a CCTV of Reynolds getting out of a Tesla at Dover Priory station. 'That's worth well over a hundred grand.'

'And it's still there?'

'Forensics brought it in on a low-loader, the tech boys are going nuts over it.'

'So that leaves us with —'

The buzzer on the intercom cut in before she could finish her sentence.

'Delivery? I thought you were cooking.'

Marshall got up, looking slightly embarrassed. 'I should have mentioned, I invited someone else.'

Biggs tried to feign disappointment, but he couldn't carry it off. 'As long as he's hot.'

'Hi, yes, please come up,' she said into the entry phone.

Professor Gresham stood in the doorway, holding a bottle in one hand and an umbrella in the other.

'Good evening,' he said, handing her the wine. 'It's a Cabernet. I assumed you like red.'

'Thanks,' she said, taking it from him. The label read 'Château La Mission Haut-Brion, 2009', it looked expensive. 'Come in.'

He walked into the room, took off his coat and looked around awkwardly for somewhere to hang it. Marshall took it from him, inadvertently catching the scent of his cologne and momentarily forgetting that Biggs was still sitting on the sofa.

'You have company?' Gresham observed, his expression giving nothing away.

'Yes, this is Detective Constable Biggs, you remember he came to your lecture.'

'Ah, yes,' he said, going over to shake Biggs's hand. 'Pleasure to see you again.'

There was an awkward tension, as if two ex-boyfriends were meeting for the first time.

'Hi,' Biggs said, giving Marshall a knowing look. 'You should be honoured. She's going to cook.'

'Is she?' The professor said with a wry smile, his eyes distracted by the wall of photos. 'Are those the crime scene photographs?'

'They are,' Marshall said. 'Biggs, why don't you take the professor through them while I start on the food?' Giving Biggs a hard stare that said *play nice.*

'Okay.'

'Would you like a drink?' she asked Gresham.

'Let it breathe for a while,' he replied, walking over to the images of the first murder. 'Was this in a church?'

Marshall left them to it and went into the kitchen. She wasn't sure what had made her invite Gresham over. Anj was right, of course, there was something sexy about him. The kind of thing that made her feel nervous and unsure, like a teenager. Taking out the ingredients for the meal, she tried to ignore the butterflies that were stirring inside her.

'This church was one of the only buildings to survive the Great Fire,' Gresham said, 'and the way she's posed, like a penitent woman seeking forgiveness in the eyes of God.'

Biggs looked impressed. 'She was having an affair.'

'The murderer knew this?'

'He did.'

'And he removed her tongue?'

Ten minutes later, Marshall walked in with a glass of wine and a beer, she handed the glass to the professor and the bottle to Biggs.

'How's it going?'

Closing his eyes Gresham rolled the wine around in the glass before sniffing the bouquet like a connoisseur and taking a sip. She did the same. The wine was incredible, it tasted of warm summer days and cherries.

'"The mouth of the just bringeth forth wisdom: but the froward tongue shall be cut out." Proverbs 10:31,' the professor quoted. 'A frequent punishment in early biblical times, for slander or bearing false witness. I think he was making her ask for absolution.' He pointed towards Melanie. 'For something she said, or perhaps not said.'

Biggs stood by the images of the burned body. 'And Reynolds was marked with fire and punished for something he had seen. His eyes were cut out.'

Gresham went to the photo of the bloody circle above the cistern at The Shard. 'Salt.' He tapped on the symbol. 'Have you found the third victim?'

Marshall shook her head. 'No.'

'What about the body they pulled from the river?' Biggs asked, staring at the photo of the hands.

'That is the symbol for water — the inverse of fire.'

Marshall shook her head. 'We're pretty sure that's not Samantha Pullman. We're just waiting for DNA to confirm it.'

'Pullman?' The professor asked. 'The daughter of the peer? The one in the news?'

'Yes, she was abducted from The Shard last Friday.'

Gresham pondered over the images, taking sips of the wine. Marshall watched him, wondering what was going on inside that brilliant mind. Would he find a pattern that she had missed? The only thing she knew for certain was that the body count was at three with a possible fourth yet to be found, which meant it was now classified as a serial killing and that meant a whole world of pain for their department.

'Does she have any connection to the other two victims?'

'Not that we're aware of.'

'He isn't choosing them at random,' the professor said, pointing at the images of Melanie and Reynolds. 'The way they died is part of some personal ritual. As I've told you before, your murderer is on a journey. These people have some relevance to him, or his past. He is trying to cleanse himself.'

She served them a beef bourguignon with mashed potatoes and tender-stem broccoli. It was the first real meal she had made since James had left and it felt good to be sitting around the table chatting and eating. The professor seemed to relax a little after the second glass of wine and Biggs discovered that they both had studied at the same college in Oxford, Christchurch. Which meant they passed the next hour trading stories about the various pubs they frequented.

Biggs made his excuses after the meal and left. There was a wicked glint in his eye when he said goodbye at the door.

She returned to find the professor standing out on the balcony.

'The Royal Hospital,' he said, looking out over the river at Greenwich Naval College. 'One of Wren's masterpieces. Did you know the palace that preceded it was the birthplace of Henry VIII and Elizabeth I?'

'My father was never a big fan of Wren's Heavenly Mansions,' Marshall replied.

Gresham chuckled, it was a deep warm sound. 'I haven't met many critics of his work.'

'He was a postmodernist.'

'Not a fan of English Baroque?'

She smiled at the memory of dragging him around the "Fairy castles" of London. 'No, I used to make him take me to St Paul's every Christmas.'

Gresham turned back towards her. 'He sounds like a good man.'

'He was.'

'When did he die?'

Marshall realised then that she was talking about him in the past tense.

'He hasn't,' she replied, her mood darkening. 'He's got dementia.'

The connection between them passed and they both stepped back from the moment.

He looked at his watch. 'It's late. I should go.'

She nodded and went to get his coat.

49

THE MONEY

Island Gardens. Friday, December 13. 07:30

Marshall was woken by the buzz of her phone.

Half-asleep, she reached out from under the duvet and tapped it, assuming it was her alarm.

The droning continued.

She took it from the bedside table and pulled it under the covers. It was James.

'Hi,' she said, her voice deep and husky from the wine.

'Heavy night?' he asked.

'Heavy painkillers,' she lied.

'Yeah, I heard you got caught up in something bad. You okay?'

'Bored. They won't let me back on the job until I've seen the doc.'

They both knew why she hadn't been to see a doctor. The last time had been when she'd lost the baby.

'Anyway,' he said, changing the subject. 'I've found

something on those bank accounts you sent me. I think you're going to like this.'

'Wait!' she snapped, putting him on speaker and scrabbling around in her drawer for a notebook and pen. 'Okay go.'

'So, five years ago, both of those accounts were paid large sums of money by separate off-shore holding companies. They were nothing but shells, and it took a while to find out who was behind them. They were hidden well, with multiple legal entities in various countries all registered to other companies. A couple of which we've been watching for some time. Ukrainian businesses fronting Russian mafia interests, that kind of thing. Anyway, there is one name that came up more than once. Paxton Holdings, it's a conglomerate — deals mostly in military contracts.'

Marshall wrote the name down.

'Do you know who is the major shareholder in Paxton?'

'No.'

'Lord Pullman.'

'What!' she exclaimed, picking up the phone. 'Samantha's dad?'

'Yes. The Right Honourable himself.'

It was the first tangible connection they'd got between the victims, but it made no sense. *Why would Pullman pay the first two victims a considerable sum of money, and then have them killed five years later?* Unless...

'Do you think this is some kind of extortion gang? Someone knew that he's willing to pay to keep his reputation?' she asked.

James was silent for a few seconds. 'I don't know Pip. He's got some very rich and powerful friends. It wouldn't surprise me if he hasn't made a few enemies along the way.'

'So what did he pay them for?' Marshall said mostly to

herself. 'Whatever it was, I'm betting it has something to do with his daughter.'

She wrote the victims' names onto the page, putting Samantha at the centre. Circling it a couple of times and connecting them together.

'Daddy got you out of some serious shit, didn't he?'

'Pippa.'

'Yes.'

'Be careful. Pullman doesn't mess around. He's got friends in very high places. He plays golf with the Chief Constable for fuck's sake.'

50

DOCTOR

Tooting, London. Friday, December 13. 09:00

Doctor Bell was an older woman in her late fifties. Marshall had been going to see her since they had moved to Tooting five years ago.

She was a friendly, if rather stern Scottish woman with a very frank bedside manner, which Marshall liked. There was no dressing up of the facts, she told it straight.

'You've had quite a year of it,' Bell said, flicking the pen torch in and out of Marshall's line of vision.

'I've had worse.'

The doctor frowned over her half-moon spectacles. 'I doubt that. Losing a baby is one of the hardest tragedies any woman has to overcome. You were supposed to take time off to recuperate not put yourself in harm's way.' She removed the blood pressure cuff from Marshall's arm and went back behind her desk.

Marshall rolled down her sleeve. 'Work takes my mind off it.'

Bell typed her notes into the computer. 'But it doesn't

allow you to heal the psychological damage. You can't just bottle up these emotions forever, they need to be expressed.'

Let's not get started on what's happening with dad, Marshall thought, pushing the sudden pang of grief to the back of her mind. 'I just need you to certify that I am physically fit for duty.'

Doctor Bell sighed. 'Well, physically you're fine. There's no sign of any concussion, but being fit for duty does not just relate to your physical health.'

She opened up another window on her PC and scrolled down through a list of names.

'I'm going to recommend you return to active duty on the proviso that you have some counselling. There's one lady I have in mind, she's very good — specialises in child bereavement.'

The doctor hit a key and the printer sprung to life.

Marshall was about to protest that nobody had died, when it struck her. Even though the foetus had only been nine weeks old, too early even to feel its heart beating, it was a living thing. She'd never thought of it in that way before and she didn't want to now.

The doctor handed her the printout with a name, address and time.

'I've made you an appointment for next Thursday at two. Do not misunderstand detective, this is a requirement of your return to active duty.'

Marshall nodded and took the paper.

51

HOUSE OF LORDS

Houses of Parliament, Westminster. Friday, December 13. 11:00

Walking into the central lobby, Marshall realised how formidable the Houses of Parliament really were. The grandeur of the interior took her breath away. Her father would have hated it, gothic revivalism always put him in a bad mood.

Politics was never her strong point, but it was hard to avoid in the police; crime was a very political topic and the Government weren't making their job any easier with their funding cuts. Will used to wind her up by pretending that she was secretly a radical socialist, adamant that she was hatching some cunning plan to remove the royalty and the capitalists when the revolution came. She used to love the way his mind worked — he saw the world in such a very different way.

Turning right, she followed the signs towards the House of Lords. She walked along the Peers Corridor where members of the public sat patiently on red leather benches waiting to enter the public gallery.

Reaching the Peers Lobby, Marshall found herself at the golden arch that lead into the Lords debating chamber. It wasn't in session and she had to stop herself from walking in to take a look.

A stern-faced guard stood at the entrance to the Moses Room. She showed him her warrant card and he opened the door, ushering her through into a long, oak-panelled corridor with a sumptuous red carpet.

A clerk in black robes appeared from behind a wooden door. 'Detective Sergeant Marshall?'

She nodded.

'Please follow me.'

The clerk took her through a maze of corridors and up a flight of stone stairs. It was like a scene from Harry Potter. Every inch of the building had been designed to invoke wonder and power.

'Please wait here,' the clerk instructed, pointing at a leather chair and disappearing through yet another ornately carved door.

Marshall sat and looked along the long passage. The half-panelled walls were decorated with gilt-framed paintings of old members of the house. She felt a little intimidated sitting beside some of the most influential men in Britain's history while they stared down at her in their ermine robes.

Her phone buzzed. It was a message from her mother.

'Dad's ok. Coming home tomorrow. x'

Although it was a relief to know he was recovering, part of her wished he would simply fall asleep and never wake up. It would spare her mother the strain of having to care for him.

The door opened. 'Lord Pullman will see you now.'

The committee room was small, nothing like the ones she had seen on the television when some banker would be hauled in front of a select group of peers.

At the other end of a long mahogany table stood Lord Pullman. He was staring out of the window. He was lean, with a sharp profile and the dark piercing eyes of a hawk. He wore a dark blue suit, white shirt and tie. His greying hair was slicked back like a trader from Wall Street *or a sixties gangster*.

'Detective Sergeant Marshall,' he greeted her in a clipped public school accent. 'I have very little time. They've called an extraordinary session for the second reading of the Madigan bill.'

She nodded. 'It's about your daughter.'

'Yes, so you said in your message. I take it you have new information?'

'I believe she's still alive.'

He frowned, his eyes hardening. 'How can you be sure? Detective Inspector Salazar informed me that she was pulled out of the river two days ago.'

'That wasn't Samantha, sir.'

The news seemed to take a second to filter through to his impassive face. His eyebrows relaxed a little and he motioned for her to sit.

They took chairs on opposite sides of the table. Pullman unbuttoned his jacket and placed his hands on the table, locking the fingers together.

'How is it that I haven't been informed of this new information?' he asked, his tone cold and unemotional.

'I've just come from the pathologist.'

'And what evidence did they have to prove that this poor woman isn't Samantha?'

Marshall thought it was wise not to mention the alchemical symbols and chose the simplest explanation. 'The contents of her stomach don't match the meal she was eating at the Oblix.'

'I see,' he said, still unmoved by the revelation.

Marshall had dealt with enough grieving parents in her career to know that this was not a normal reaction. Most hold on to any glimmer of hope, any potential mistake that could have led to a wrongful identification. He should have been overjoyed.

'Weren't you one of the officers that was injured at Harbour Quay?'

'I was, but I've recovered.'

'Why do you think he took her?'

'I'm sorry, but I can't discuss an ongoing investigation.'

He nodded. 'Of course, my apologies. Did you know that site was acquired by one of my property companies?'

Marshall took out her notebook. 'Would that be Paxton Holdings?'

Pullman steepled his hands, bringing them up to his nose.

'No, it would not.'

'But you are the Chairman of Paxton?'

'I am. Amongst many others, you can find them listed in the directory of member's interests.'

He's unshakeable, she thought. *At no point has he dropped his guard.*

Marshall went for a direct question. 'It's just that we've

found payments made to two of the other victims by companies connected to Paxton Holdings.'

'Have you? How interesting. I suppose you believe that I am being blackmailed for the return of my daughter?'

'Are you?' she asked bluntly.

He shook his head. 'I don't believe in paying ransoms Detective Sergeant. It's a sign of weakness. Samantha would have been a target for most of her life. Whoever has her now has not approached me. Although this is not the first time she's faked her disappearance, sometimes I believe she does it for attention.'

'You think she's hiding?' Marshall said, trying to mask the disbelief in her voice.

His shoulders relaxed a little and he opened his hands. 'Samantha is an addict. Her motives are somewhat unpredictable. I resigned myself to that fact a long time ago. Of course I'm glad to hear that she's not dead.' He looked at his watch and stood up. 'If you'll excuse me I must return to the House.'

'And the payments to the other victims?'

'Give your card to the clerk and I'll have one of my assistants look into it.'

The clerk hovered by the door waiting to escort her out.

52

SATURDAY

West Middlesex Hospital. Saturday, December 14. 11:00

Her mother was waiting at the front door. She looked as if she was going on holiday; wearing her best coat and carrying a small travel suitcase.

Marshall made the taxi wait while she went to help her put the case in the boot.

'I didn't know what to bring,' she explained. 'I packed his suit. The one he wore at your cousin's wedding, and his good shoes. You know how much he likes his brogues.'

The ride to the hospital took another twenty minutes and her mother spent the entire journey talking through a mental shopping list of things she had to do when he came home. It was her way of controlling the situation, to worry about the little things so they didn't have time to focus on the real issue.

Marshall held her hand and let her talk, letting her

mother's voice distract her from all the bad thoughts she was having.

The ward was quiet. Visiting didn't start for another hour and when they reached his room they found a gathering of white coats around her father's bed. Her mother gripped Marshall's hand tightly.

'Mrs Marshall,' the consultant greeted her with the well practised look of impassivity.

Her father had suffered another stroke.

After the doctors had left, they sat quietly beside his bed watching him sleep. There was nothing to say, the consultant had explained he was suffering from something called Atrial Fibrillation. The upper chambers of his heart were not pumping efficiently and so blood clots were forming.

One of them had blocked an artery feeding his brain, starving it of oxygen.

'Do you think they will let him come home today?' her mother had asked, not understanding the implications of what the doctor had told her.

'No Mum,' Marshall said, her voice tight from holding back the emotion. 'He's too ill. This is the best place for him.'

Her mother nodded, eyes filling with tears. 'I've bought a nice piece of beef. Who'll eat that now?'

A nurse arrived and checked her father's pulse and blood pressure.

He stirred as she finished the last of her observations.

'Hello Pip,' he said, half of his face breaking into a smile. 'I didn't know you were coming.'

'Hi Dad,' she replied, taking his hand.

'How have you been?' He spoke with a lisp, his lips trying to form the words and failing.

Marshall didn't know where to begin, the last few weeks had been a nightmare and she had little other news that didn't involve work.

'I saw Anj last week. She's gone off to Singapore.'

'Anj, I liked Anj. She was always a bit of a tearaway. Your mother hated her,' he said raising one eyebrow.

Marshall turned to her mother, who was doing her best not to cry.

'She said to say hello.'

'How is school? Have you done your homework?'

This was not the first conversation with him that slipped back into the past. Over the last year, his brain seemed to have lost its grip on time. Marshall learned early on that it was better to just go with it.

'Good. I got an A for my physics essay. You know the one about the solar system.'

He nodded and closed his eyes. 'You've always loved the stars.'

Her father had bought her a ninety-millimetre refractor telescope for her twelfth birthday. It was not the usual kind of present for a girl on the brink of becoming a teenager, but she loved it all the same. They would spend hours together in the garden during the evenings staring up at the craters of the moon, or the divisions of Saturn's rings.

'I hated that thing,' her mother muttered.

'I know. Where is it now?'

'In the shed. Along with all his other half-finished projects.'

Her father collected stuff that other people would throw away. Notorious for diving into skips and pulling out random junk and pieces of wood. 'You never know when they might come in handy,' he would say. There were three sheds in their garden, each one filled with half-repaired lawnmowers he had acquired or old chests of drawers filled with tins and jars of nuts and bolts.

'His bloody sheds,' her mother said, gripping his hand. 'What am I going to do with all that stuff?'

53

SUNDAY

Harbour Quay, Docklands. Sunday, December 15. 11:00

The van had been removed from the site. All that was left was a darkened shadow in the dirt where the fire had scorched the earth.

Marshall ducked under the police tape and knelt beside the burned ground. Images of the final moments before Ford and Palmer opened the back doors flashed through her mind. The forensics report had said that the chemicals used in the incendiary device were not standard. That the bomb maker must have had military experience. It was not something you could just put together from high street products.

Why did you bring her here? She asked herself.

Marshall stood up and surveyed the surrounding area. The building site was bordered on three sides by water. To the east was the Thames, the north was the Blackwall Basin and looking south she could see the old dock cranes standing redundant, their arms left pointing up towards the clouds. They still bore the signs of Stothert & Pitt, the engineering firm who built them, based in Bath. Her grandfather had worked there for most of his life.

There were only two routes out of the quay: along the A1206 into Tower Hamlets or west towards the towering business district of Canary Wharf.

He would have been carrying her, she thought, *and it would have been dark.*

She tried to imagine what it would have been like, pulling the limp body of Samantha out of the back of the van and hoisting her over his shoulder. Unless he had another car somewhere close by, he wouldn't have been able to take her far, no matter how fit he was.

Or maybe he had a boat, she wondered, looking over at the narrow boats moored in the Blackwall Basin.

Marshall walked along the waterside and up the stairs onto the roundabout at Trafalgar Way. The boats below her wallowed in the still, oil-slicked water, like sleeping whales waiting to be woken.

Stepping down onto the floating quay, an old man appeared from a small blue cabin. His coat bore the badge of the London Port Authority.

'Can I help you love?'

'Police,' she said, holding up her warrant card.

He grabbed an old cloth and wiped his oily hands before taking it from her.

'Detective Sergeant Marshall,' he read before handing it back to her. 'City Police, bit out of your area aren't you?'

'I'm following up on an incident.' She nodded towards Harbour Quay. 'At the construction site.'

'Bad business,' he said, 'I heard two coppers died.'

'Yes. Tell me, are all of these boats occupied?'

He shrugged. 'Hard to say for sure. Most of them keep to themselves. Private like.'

'Has anyone left in the last week?'

'They come and go all the time. You looking for someone?'

'Man and a woman, late thirties maybe early forties.'

The port officer sucked air in through his teeth, his eyes scanning over the marina as he did some kind of mental inventory. 'Seventy footer left last Monday. Can't say who was on board but they'd paid for another two weeks.'

'Can you give me their details.'

'Sure,' he said, disappearing back into the cabin.

Marshall called Biggs.

'Hey, I've got a lead on a boat leaving Blackwall Basin the day after the explosion, can you follow it up?'

The port officer reappeared and handed her the details which she read out to Biggs.

54

MAYBERRY

Wood Street Police Station, London. Monday, December 16. 12:00

Jonathan Mayberry shifted uncomfortably in his seat while Biggs prepared the tape.

Marshall watched him closely, studying the small facial ticks and hand movements. He was a fascinating subject, the tattoos on his fingers spoke of time spent in jail, as did the small bird on his neck. He had a long, straggly beard and wiry, matted hair. He looked as if he had been sleeping rough for months, but they had traced him to a bail hostel in Battersea.

'You got a fag?' he asked.

'You can't smoke in here Mr Mayberry.'

He shrugged. 'For later?'

She shook her head.

Biggs began the interview. 'Jonathan Mayberry.'

'Yes.'

'Can you confirm that you worked at Monument ticket office during the period 2017 to 2018?'

He screwed up his eyes and counted with his fingers against his thumb. 'Yeah. June 2018. That little fucker Parnell kicked me out in the middle of the tourist season.'

'He sacked you for running private tours after hours. Correct?'

'Is that what he says?'

'It is.'

'Wanker.'

Marshall leaned forward. 'Did you ever make a copy of the key?'

Mayberry laughed. 'Have you seen it? Who do you know could make a copy of that thing? It's a bloody antique.'

'Where were you on the night of the second of December?'

He licked his finger and pretended to open a diary, flicking through the invisible pages. 'Let me see. That would have been a Tuesday?'

'Monday,' Biggs corrected him.

'I was selling the Big Issue on the Strand.'

'Can anyone corroborate that?'

He sneered, crossing his arms. 'No one you'd believe.'

It was then that Marshall noticed the tattoos on his forearms. They were a line of symbols that looked similar to alchemical elements.

'Where did you get those?'

'Navy, served seven years. Much good it did me.'

'Do you know what they mean?'

'Had them done in Singapore one night, too drunk to remember why. They're supposed to bring good fortune. Can't say that I have noticed any.'

'Would you mind if we took a photo?' Biggs asked, taking out his phone.

Mayberry looked at him suspiciously. 'Tell me why you dragged me in here first.'

'There was a fire, at Monument, somebody died.'

His tone changed. 'And you think it was me because I used to let a few tourists in after hours?'

Marshall shook her head. 'We're just following all possible leads.'

'There are at least two others with keys to that place.'

'And we're speaking to them too.'

'Don't forget Parnell, he likes to play the big man, but he's dodgy as fuck.'

'Dodgy how?' Biggs asked.

Mayberry sneered. 'Likes 'em young. If you know what I mean.'

She ignored him, taking out a photograph of Samantha. 'Have you ever met this woman?' She asked, holding it up.

He leaned forward and studied it then shook his head. 'Nah, I'd remember a posh tart like that.'

The door opened and Salazar stepped in. 'DS Marshall, a word if you please.'

'I'm taking over the interview,' the DI said when they were outside.

Of course you are.

'There's little more than circumstantial on him.'

'Have you seen his record? Assault, GBH and two charges of intent to supply. He knows the streets and had access to Monument.'

'But, it doesn't tell us why he did it.'

'Leave that to me,' Salazar said smugly, opening the door. 'Donovan wants to see you.'

55

DONOVAN

Wood Street Police Station, London. Monday, December 16. 12:30

Donovan was on a call.

While Marshall waited outside his office, she could see the colour rising in his cheeks. She wondered if her visit to Lord Pullman had rattled some cages.

Biggs came back to his desk.

'Hey, did you get anything on that narrow boat at Blackwall Basin?'

He shook his head. 'They're not like cars, no ANPR, bloody thing could take weeks to surface.'

'Put Baxter on it.'

The DCI finally put the phone down and rubbed his hands over his face, he looked like a man who'd just been told he had terminal cancer.

He looked up and waved for her to come in.

'That was the Chief Constable,' he began. 'Apparently

Lord Pullman was less than happy with your line of questioning.'

She was pleased, if Pullman had just ignored her then she wasn't a threat. It may have damaged her future career prospects but it was worth it.

'Tell me exactly why we're bothering this peer of the realm and a grieving father?'

'Firstly, I don't think Samantha's dead, and second it's a bit of a coincidence that one of his shell companies paid off the first two victims,' Marshall said defiantly.

Donovan's stern expression softened a little.

'And what did he say when you confronted him about that?'

'He denied all knowledge, said he'd get one of his assistants to look into it.'

'Of course he fucking did. Then he went and complained to the Chief and half of the fucking rotary club. Do you think he's really involved?'

'Yes, sir,' she answered.

'And this Mayberry. Where does he fit into this conspiracy of yours?'

'I don't think he does.'

Donovan grimaced as he got up. Kneading his fist into the small of his back. 'DI Salazar has other ideas.'

'I know, but he doesn't fit the profile. He's not a chemist and he's never heard of Samantha Pullman.'

'Well he's hardly likely to admit it is he? Have you thought that there might be more than one of them?'

She hadn't, serial killers generally worked alone. The idea that this was some kind of collaboration was an option she hadn't considered, but it did explain why Sam's abduction was out of kilter with the others.

'Let's tread a little more carefully. I'm fine with you

digging around in Pullman's affairs, but start with NCA and Fraud. See if there have been any investigations into any of his other companies.'

'Already have Guv, we're just waiting for their report.'

Donovan smiled and she saw there was a glint in his eye. Marshall knew the look too well, it meant he was getting a taste for the hunt — things were finally starting to fall into place.

He rolled up his sleeves. 'So where are we with our mermaid?'

'Nothing yet, still waiting on DNA.'

'And the hard drive from Reynolds?'

'Going to pay data retrieval a visit this afternoon,' Marshall replied.

'Good. Let's assume Samantha Pullman is still alive and that Mayberry isn't working alone. Get out there and find me enough to nail these sick fuckers to the wall.'

56

DATA RETRIEVAL

Wood Street Police Station, London. Monday, December 16. 13:30

Four of the hard drives from Reynolds's server were sitting upright in cradles on Frazer's desk.

He looked like he hadn't slept in three days, and he smelled like it too.

Lines of code were continuously scrolling up the screen as his system tried to decrypt the data stored on the disk.

'It's military-grade encryption,' he said.

'What does that mean?' Marshall asked, crossing her arms. Frazer had a terrible habit of talking to her breasts instead of her face.

'It's the kind of thing the SAS put into their helicopters and laptops. So if they go down behind enemy lines they can leave their shit behind knowing that the enemy will never be able to crack it.'

'So we're not going to get into it?'

Frazer shook his head. 'Not in this century, not without the password.' He pointed at the screen. 'This is a dictionary attack, brutal but usually effective. Most people have one password that they use for everything. Their birthday or a pet's name, all pretty guessable. But this guy is SecOps, he probably changed it every thirty days and used a strong combination of upper and lower case characters or possibly an authentication app on his mobile.'

'There was no sign of his phone at the scene.'

'Shame, probably would have been easier to hack than this. Whatever's on here, he wanted to make sure no one ever got access to it without his consent.'

'How did you get on with the internet service provider?'

Frazer turned his chair to another terminal and brought up a log of Reynolds internet traffic. It was a long list of IP addresses, that much Marshall could recognise.

'They're mostly routed through VPNs or proxies. The only legit traffic was encrypted to his email and some streaming stuff on Netflix.'

Marshall sat down in a chair and watched the lights blinking on the rack of servers. Whatever Reynolds had been doing it was bound to be illegal. No one went to this much trouble to hide their private life, unless they were into child porn or snuff movies.

'According to the locals, he used to have wild, noisy parties. Yet work said he had no friends, what does that say to you?'

Frazer shrugged, unplugging one of the drives. 'Sounds pretty normal to me.'

'Like he was leading a double life.'

'Or he wanted to maintain a good work-life balance.'

Marshall could see that Frazer was taking this way too personally.

'What about the car they found at the station?'

'The Tesla?' Frazer's eyes lit up. 'Now that's one cool

piece of shit. It's a second-gen Roadster. The specs say it can do nought to sixty in one-point-nine seconds. Will set you back two-hundred and fifty-thousand without the upgrades.'

Marshall tried to look impressed but failed. 'Does it have its own GPS?'

For once he didn't have the answer. Frazer pulled up a page from the Tesla website and scrolled down to the page. 'It has two SIM cards, one for telematics and software updates, and the other is for user data.'

'And that's good?'

Frazer was already out of his seat and heading for the stairs. 'I'll let you know when I've taken the thing apart.'

57

BENJAMIN SYKES

Temple Underground Station, London. Monday, December 16. 18:00

T*here you are. The one who walks between the two worlds.*

Benjamin Sykes waits at the far end of the station. It is rush hour and the westbound platform is crowded with business men and women squinting into the pale light of their phones or staring at the signage anxiously awaiting the arrival of the next train.

No one looks at each other.

He walks between them and they part to let him pass. They are like the damned. Their vacant faces transfixed by images of the lives they wish they had. He sees their pain so clearly. The ones who spend every day wishing for the nightmare to be over, to surrender to the void, but who never quite have the courage to step beyond the yellow line.

A low rumble echoes along the darkened tunnel as he stands beside Sykes.

Turning to the woman next to him, he smiles. She reciprocates instinctively, but he can see there is no real sincerity beneath those thin lips. Her eyes are full of regret, she begs to be released.

It is nothing more than a gentle nudge and she loses her balance, falling into the path of the oncoming train.

He hears Sykes scream over the screech of the brakes and turns towards him. In the ensuing chaos, he drives the needle into the side of the man's neck.

58

ALDWYCH

Aldwych Underground Station, London. Tuesday, December 17. 03:00

The maintenance crew for tunnel twelve were running behind schedule. It was three in the morning and the crew had to be finished by five-thirty so that the power could be turned back on.

Dave Linden switched on the helmet lamp and watched the rats scatter into the shadows as he made his way down to the secondary junction. These were the older, deeper tunnels, the ones that the commuters never got to see. Decommissioned tracks leading to dead stations, it was like a piece of history down there. Frozen in time and forgotten.

Along the tunnel, he could hear the voices of the other engineers on his team. They had gone ahead with the equipment while he double-checked the work order.

His walkie-talkie hissed with static, but he ignored it. The old lags used to say the radios could pick up the sounds of the dead. He knew they were just old wives' tales, and this crew were notorious for playing tricks. The tunnels below

Temple were not great for anyone with a nervous disposition, there were supposed to be more than one mass grave down here.

Dave didn't care, he'd seen it all. Bodies on the tracks, the homeless junkies who had just crawled in to find somewhere quiet to die. It was nothing compared to what he had seen on his last tour, anything was easier to deal with than that.

He was ex-army, Royal Engineers, and they had been sent into Northern Iraq to clear IEDs. Nothing could prepare you for what happened out there — bodies weren't supposed to come apart like that. Nobody was supposed to witness that kind of carnage.

'Sarge!' One of the guys called out from the dark. The rank had stuck even after he had left the service.

'Coming,' he responded.

'Someone's been screwing with the equipment.'

His old sapper instincts kicked in. 'Don't touch nothing.'

59

TEMPLE

Temple Underground Station, London. Tuesday, December 17. 08:00

Following the station manager along the platform, they came to a small metal door covered in the high voltage safety warnings. Marshall tried not to look down onto the tracks where the woman had fallen, but she did all the same — it was human nature to stare into the abyss. She shuddered at the thought of falling under those metal wheels, the clean-up crew had been very efficient, there was nothing left on the tracks except for a few patches of sand.

As if it never happened.

At first, the Transport Police had logged it as a suicide, but later the CCTV showed them something else. It was a perfect diversionary tactic; no one paid any attention to the passenger collapsing or the member of staff pulling him through the access hatch, they were all too busy running away from the accident.

Marshall gave her name to the uniformed officer and he

copied it into the log. Behind him she could see into the badly-lit passageway. It looked like they were about to enter the bowels of hell.

After the call from the Chief, Donovan had pulled rank and opted to lead on this case.

Salazar had kept Mayberry in for questioning and didn't want to waste any of her precious twenty-four hours.

Marshall was glad to be working with Donovan. He had good natural instincts and, contrary to his rather tired-looking face, a very sharp mind. The DCI hunched a little as he stepped through into the dingy passage. He was a big man, over six foot tall, but years of flying a desk had thickened his waistline. She noticed him breathing hard after they walked down the stairs at Temple. It was a long way down and the escalators had been stopped as a matter of procedure. The old man was sweating by the time they reached the platform.

Making their way down the access tunnel felt like walking into the inner workings of a giant machine. The air was hot and tasted of grease and dust, reminding Marshall of her grandfather's garage.

There were strange noises: high-pitched screeching of trains passing overhead and the mosquito-like buzz of electricity making the hairs on her neck stand on end, but worst of all was the skittering of tiny claws on cement. The thought of rats made Marshall's skin crawl. When the lights flickered out every couple of minutes, she could have sworn things were climbing over her feet.

Eventually they walked out onto Aldwych station and into another time.

. . .

The manager had explained that the station had been closed down in 1994. Sealing it like a time capsule. There were tattered old posters advertising Blur and Radiohead albums, bands that she was listening to when she was ten. Beneath them she could still see the original Edwardian tiled walls, unchanged from the times when the station was used as an air raid shelter during the Blitz.

'This way,' said the manager, stepping down onto the empty tracks and making for the entrance to the tunnel. 'It's okay, the power's off.'

Ahead of them, Marshall could see the bright LED lamps of the SOCOs. The tunnel was filled with equipment, cable drums and wooden crates were stacked next to large plastic barrels. She noticed the forensics team weren't wearing their usual white disposable suits, instead they lumbered around in cumbersome hazmat gear like deep sea divers. The rotund figure of Gates was striding towards them, carrying something in a glass vial and waving for them to stop.

'The repair crew reported something wrong with the barrels,' the manager explained. 'One of them was ex-army, served in Iraq clearing IEDs. He took one look at the way the barrels had been arranged and called it in.'

Gates pulled off the gas mask with his free hand. His head was covered in beads of sweat, plastering his frizzy hair to his scalp.

'Is it safe?' Donovan asked, looking over at the site.

The pathologist nodded. 'Bomb squad left with counter terrorism half an hour ago. There's no sign of any explosives, but there is something interesting about that one.'

He pointed at one of the larger plastic drums. There was an alchemical symbol stencilled over its label.

Gates held up the vial, it was half full of a yellowish

liquid. 'Initial tests are pointing towards hydrofluoric acid so we're not taking any chances. It's terrible stuff, highly corrosive to human tissue — a lungful of the gas will give you a fatal pulmonary edema in minutes.'

His team were adjusting one of the lamps to point directly through the translucent blue plastic barrel. When they switched it on they could see the outline of a body inside.

'Bollocks!' Gates swore.

'What is it?'

'If we don't get him out in the next few hours there won't be anything left of him to identify.'

60

ALCHEMIST

Victoria Embankment Gardens, London. Tuesday, December 17. 10:00

There was a message on Marshall's phone when she reached street level.

It was a voicemail from Anj.

'Hi honey, just wanted to say thanks for the other night. It was great to catch up. Listen, I remembered something else about Samantha Pullman, not sure it will be any use, but anyway. She used to hangout with a bunch of hedge fund wankers. You know the types, too much money and no style. We went to one of their parties once, at the Welbeck. There was a guy there, a broker, I can't remember his name, but everyone referred to him as "The Alchemist", something to do with him being able to turn everything he touched into gold, or some macho bullshit like that. Samantha sold them a shit load of coke, kept her in silk panties after daddy cut off her allowance.' Anj was interrupted by the sound of a taxi blaring its horn.

'I'm coming, two minutes,' she told the cab, repeating it again in Italian.

'Have to go babe. The club was in the city, bloody exclusive place. Next to Rothschilds. Probably isn't there any more, but you never know. Those fuckers thought they were immortal. But hey didn't we all back in those days! Ciao.'

Marshall listened to the message twice.

She turned back towards the station and met Donovan coming out. His face was flushed pink and he was panting heavily. 'Where are you going?'

'I've got to go.'

'Where?'

'New lead on Samantha.'

'Shouldn't we let PDP deal with that?'

'Not until I've checked it out,' she said, walking towards the ticket barrier and flashing her warrant card.

Donovan watched her go. 'I'm getting too old for this shit.'

61

WALBROOK

Bond Court, London. Tuesday, December 17. 11:00

The Welbeck Club was a small red-brick house wedged in between the glass and steel office buildings of the Rothschilds Bank, St Stephen's church and a shopping mall. It was a cute Queen Anne style building that was so out-of-place that it looked as though it had been dropped in by some American tycoon as a joke.

She called Biggs as she walked down Bond Court towards it.

'Hi boss, how did it go at Temple?'

'It's definitely him. Check the CCTV from the platform, the moment just before the woman fell under the train. It's going to be the same guy.'

'Not Mayberry then?'

'No, not fucking Mayberry. This one has all the usual hallmarks. Listen, I've got a new lead on Samantha. A friend of mine told me there was an exclusive club she used to supply with Class A. I'm on my way there now.'

'Sounds like an interesting friend.'

'Oh she is. Get hold of the professor and see if there are any alchemical links to solvents. Looks like he was trying to dissolve his victim this time.'

'Good morning, ma'am,' said the immaculately dressed concierge, his expression a well-rehearsed mixture of welcoming smile and humble servitude.

The reception was a quirky room, like walking into the hallway of someone's home. There was a grandfather clock noisily marking time in the corner and a chintzy armchair next to a fireplace.

'DS Marshall,' she said, showing her warrant card. 'I'm investigating the disappearance of Samantha Pullman.'

The receptionist's smile twisted away and a phone appeared in his hand almost instantly.

'One moment,' he said, raising a finger. 'The police are here. They want to talk about Ms Pullman.'

There was a short silence while he nodded and then ended the call.

'My manager will be happy to assist you. Please follow me.'

He turned woodenly, like an automaton, and made his way through a series of small corridors, past a lavish dining room, bar and up a grand staircase to the first floor.

The manager's office was like something from a Jane Austen novel. It was decorated with beautiful antique furniture and gilt-framed paintings. He was in his fifties, with an air of someone who spent most of his time in the company of millionaires. While his mouth smiled as they shook hands, his eyes did not. They were full of questions and distrust.

This man knows something, Marshall thought taking a seat.

'My name is Felhoffen. Raymond informs me that you are interested in one of our members.' His accent was subtle under its public school refinement. Either German or perhaps Swiss, the phrase pitched somewhere between a question and a statement.

'Yes, Samantha Pullman.'

She watched him carefully, but there was no hint of hesitation, he would have made a damn fine poker player. She knew they wouldn't be having this conversation if he didn't have something to tell her.

'Ms Pullman's father is one of our founding members.'

No surprises there.

'We are investigating the disappearance of Samantha.' She emphasised the use of her first name, somehow the way they insisted on referring to her by her last name felt like she was already dead. 'We have reason to believe that it's linked to other members of this club.'

His expression darkened and he shook his head. 'All applicants are very carefully vetted. We pride ourselves on our selection process. One must be a senior executive of director level and be seconded by two existing members.'

This was his weak spot, the reputation of the club.

'I was informed that she attended parties at this club, with a particular group. One of whom may have gone by the title of the "The Alchemist".'

There was the nervous twitch, just below his left eye. A subtle tremor that most people would have missed.

He pursed his lips for a second, weighing up what to say next.

'I know no one by that name.'

'But you could give me a list of her associates? It may help to track her down.'

Felhoffen placed his hands on his desk, lacing his fingers together. 'I'm afraid this is a private members club. I cannot divulge such information without the appropriate documentation.'

'Why don't we speak to her father?' Marshall said, taking out her phone and scrolling through her contacts. 'I'm sure his Lordship would be very interested to hear how you're hindering my investigation.'

'I'm sure that won't be necessary.'

'So the list?'

Grudgingly, he turned to his computer and keyed something into the system.

'I hope you will convey to his Lordship how helpful the Welbeck was in assisting you.'

'Of course.'

62

SYKES

Wood Street Police Station, London. Tuesday, December 17. 14:00

Biggs was studying the CCTV from Temple station when Marshall got back to the office.

She shrugged off her coat, and pulled up a chair. 'What've you got?'

He paused the recording and tapped on the screen, enlarging the image

'There's your man. Standing next to the middle-aged woman. He's dressed like a member of staff.'

She squinted at the picture, it was fuzzy, impossible to make out his features properly.

'Is that a beard?'

'It's probably fake. He didn't have one in the footage from The Shard. Watch what happens next.'

He hit play and they watched the staff member push the woman off the platform. Marshall was relieved that the way the image was cropped meant that she didn't have to witness the death. The expressions of horror on the other passengers beside her were bad enough.

In the next chaotic seconds as the crowd began to scatter, she saw the staff member stab the man next to him with something. His body crumpled. The bearded man then appeared to pick him up under the arms and drag him through the metal service door.

'That's it,' Biggs said, tapping the space bar to pause the playback.

'Did you get a clear shot of the victim.'

'Yup. Better still, we know who he is.'

'Already?'

The constable looked very satisfied with himself. 'Face recognition got a match virtually straight away.'

'And?'

'He's one of us, an ex-copper, Ben Sykes. The Guv used to work with him.'

Marshall turned to look at Donovan's office, the door was closed which was his way of saying: 'Stay the fuck out.'

Biggs pulled up his file on his laptop.

'He started out in CID, then moved to Special Branch. Some of his stuff is classified. We know what that means.'

She did. There was a blurred line between the intelligence services and the police. Special Branch had merged into counter terrorism back in 2005, but everyone still referred to them by their old name. They worked closely with the spooks at MI5 on covert operations, which meant that most ordinary coppers had no clue about what they were doing, and as such didn't trust them.

'Sykes left the force five years ago. Went into private security as a consultant. He's worked mostly overseas for the last four. Came back a few months ago after a stint in Hong Kong.'

'Any connection with the other victims?'

'Not so far,' Biggs said, nodding towards Baxter who had just returned from lunch.

'Baxter, has Gates managed to decant the body?' Marshall asked.

Baxter, put on his reading glasses and checked his logbook. He was old school, preferring to keep a written record alongside the digital one. 'Yes, the body left Temple an hour ago. He was moved by a special containment detail to the mortuary at Westminster.'

Marshall turned back to Biggs. 'Did you get hold of Gresham?'

The DC shook his head. 'He's been in lectures all morning.'

She picked up her coat. 'I'm going to see him and then drop in on Gates.' She handed him the list of members from the club. 'These are some of Samantha's known associates. Apparently one of them used to go by the alias of "The Alchemist".'

Biggs looked at her with wide eyes. 'Alchemist?'

She smiled. 'I think one of the names on there might be our killer.'

63

ALKAHEST

King's College, London. Tuesday, December 17. 14:30

'Well, this is an unexpected pleasure,' Gresham said, waiting until the last of his students left the lecture theatre. 'People will begin to wonder.'

Marshall wasn't in the mood for small talk.

'We've got another victim. I want you to come down and tell me what you think.'

He looked at his watch. 'I have a tutorial session in thirty minutes.'

'Cancel it,' she said sternly.

'It won't make the poor devil any less dead. What's so important about this one?'

'In an hour there might not be anything left of him to identify.'

The mortuary was crowded with hazmat teams trying to manoeuvre the large barrel into the laboratory. Gates insisted they wait in the viewing gallery while he carefully directed the delicate operation of removing the body from the acid.

A manual winch was hooked up to a metal tripod and what was left of the body was slowly hoisted out of the thick, organic soup.

The corpse looked as though it had melted. The skin sloughed off him like candle wax, exposing tissue and bone in various states of dissolution.

The steel cord and hook were steaming as the acid ate through them. Men quickly doused the equipment with jets of water, inadvertently sluicing chunks of the man's body onto the floor.

'The alkahest,' whispered the stunned professor.

Marshall looked away. It was beginning to make her feel ill. 'What's that?'

'A universal solvent. Many alchemists believed there was a solution that could break down any material into its component parts. Its *Prima Materia*. The alkahest was supposed to remove all of the impurities. Some thought it could be used for medicinal purposes.'

Gates's team manipulated the rig until the remains were over the mortuary table. It was a difficult operation wearing the bulky gloves and suits. They looked like a bunch of scientists decanting an alien life form.

'Is this the last part of his Opus? The killer left this symbol on the container.' Marshall said, showing him a picture of the barrel when it was lit by the lamp. The silhouette of the body could still be seen inside it. The killer had stencilled the glyph onto the side, it was a circle that contained a triangle around a square.

. . .

The professor took the phone from her and zoomed in on the mark. 'He has one last transmutation. There should be another circle within the square.'

'And what would that involve?' Marshall said, trying not to imagine what horror awaited the next victim.

'Gold. He has to transmute base matter into gold.'

Gates made them wear gas masks before they were allowed into the lab.

The body on the table was steaming, small rivulets of body fluid pooled under the slowly dissolving corpse. Two of his team were taking photographs while another panned up and down the table with a video camera.

'You'll have to excuse them,' he said, his voice muffled through the respirator. 'We don't have a great deal of time and we need to capture as much detail as we can.'

'Was he alive when he was put into the acid?' Marshall asked.

'I doubt it. The arms and legs have been broken so that he could fit into the barrel. All of the fingers have been removed on his right hand.' Gates pointed to the stubs with a metal probe. 'And there is a hole in the back of his cranium that looks as though someone drilled into it.'

'Trepanning,' Gresham said, walking around to look at the back of the skull. 'It's one of the oldest surgical procedures. Archaeologists have found evidence of trepanation going back to the Neolithic.'

'What is it?'

'In medieval times it was thought to cure certain mental conditions, by releasing the evil spirits.'

Gates inspected the hole. 'It's over thirty millimetres and

it's very recent. The acid would have dissolved the brain tissue in seconds.'

64

SALAZAR

Wood Street Police Station, London. Tuesday, December 17. 16:00

Salazar was waiting for her when Marshall returned to the station.

'You got a minute?' she asked in an unusually friendly tone.

'Sure,' Marshall responded without thinking, following her into one of the interview rooms.

There was something odd about the way the DI was acting, like suddenly they were friends. The DI leaned against the table and smiled. Her dead eyes reminding Marshall of one of those wildlife documentaries of a cobra about to strike.

'I just wanted to have a chat, off the record.'

'Okay,' said Marshall, *this is getting weirder by the minute.*

'This Professor Gresham. I've had the press officer red-flagging something about his past, a relationship with a student.'

Marshall relaxed a little although she didn't show it. 'Yes, it was never proven. The girl dropped the charges.'

'Not the kind of thing we want associated with this case though. The last thing we need right now is to find out our so-called expert is a paedophile.'

'She was twenty-two.' Marshall said, suddenly aware that she was trying to defend him.

Salazar's eyes narrowed. 'Is there something going on between you two?'

Marshall frowned. 'No.'

Salazar waved her hand as if she wasn't really that interested. 'Doesn't matter to the gutter press, they'll twist the facts any way they can to get a story. We've got enough trouble keeping the other murders off the front page. The engineers that discovered the body at Aldwych have already posted some of the footage on Instagram.'

She took out her phone and showed Marshall a grisly video.

'Can't we have them taken down?'

The DI shook her head. 'Too late, they've already hit over fifty thousand views. No way to bury this now. We're in to damage limitation. So you need to distance yourself from Gresham. You don't want another black mark on your record.'

Marshall was confused, why was her mortal enemy trying to help her? The woman had been treating her like shit ever since she came back to work. They both knew that Salazar's position was temporary and that she was on thin ice with Donovan, the one making the decisions about whether it became permanent.

'What would you suggest?' Marshall asked, playing the submissive card, hoping that Salazar might show her hand.

'Leave all further contact to me. I want you to go back

over the Monument case. Mayberry has got himself a lawyer and stopped talking. Go and get a statement from his ex-boss, Parnell.'

Salazar stood up and straightened her jacket. 'Let's keep this to ourselves,' she added, signalling the end of the conversation.

Marshall should have seen it coming. The DI knew that she was close. The news about the so-called "Alchemist" had been their first real break. Salazar had let her do all the donkey work and now she was going to step in and take the glory.

Not fucking likely.

65

PARNELL

Stepney Causeway, London. Wednesday, December 18. 08:00

Parnell's flat was close to Commercial Road, a five minute walk from Limehouse station.

It was on Marshall's way into the office and so she was there early, hoping to catch him before he left for work.

Ogilvy House was a classic sixties tenement block overlooked by the Docklands Light Railway. The streets around it were a mixture of shuttered shopfronts and MOT garages. The old pub on the corner, The Royal Oak, had closed down, its doors secured with iron grilles and covered in graffiti.

Not the best neighbourhood, she thought as she pressed the buzzer on flat thirty-seven.

There was no answer.

She pressed thirty-six, then thirty-five.

'Hello?' An old lady's voice crackled through the intercom when she got to thirty-two.

'Hi, I've got a delivery for thirty-seven,' Marshall lied. It was a sad reflection on society that you were more likely to get someone to let you in if you were Amazon than the Police.

'I'm not sure he's in dear.'

'Can I leave it with you?'

There was a pause.

'I'm on a double yellow line.'

'All right, one moment.' The speaker went silent and a few seconds later the door latch clicked.

Marshall pulled it open and walked inside.

Thirty-seven was on the third floor. She knew better than to take the lift, even if it was working they always smelled like toilets, and the thought of getting trapped in one was enough incentive to get her up three flights of stairs.

The old lady was standing at her door when she reached the landing.

'I haven't seen him for a couple of days now,' she said, without any prompting. 'Rupert usually comes around for his tea, regular as clockwork.'

'Rupert?'

'His mother's cat. He moved in after she passed. Where's this parcel then?'

Marshall took out her warrant card. 'I'm a police officer.'

The woman squinted at it. 'No point in showing me that without my glasses, could be a library card for all I can tell.'

Number thirty-seven was directly opposite the old lady. There was a small coir mat in front of the door with the words "Welcome" burned into it. A flowerpot sat sadly beside the mat with a geranium withering inside it.

Marshall knocked loudly on the door. There was still no

answer. She bent down and looked through the letterbox into a darkened hallway.

'Do you have a spare key Mrs—'

'Winkle, Winnifred Winkle. I do dear, but I'm not sure you can just go in there.'

There was a noise, a buzzing and then the smell hit her nostrils.

Marshall let the letterbox flap fall back and stood up. 'Winnifred, would you mind getting me the key? I have a feeling Rupert is trapped in there on his own — I think I heard him crying.'

'Oh dear, yes. Wait a moment.'

While she went back into the flat, Marshall pulled out her phone and called Biggs.

'Hey, I'm at Parnell's flat. Neighbour says she hasn't seen him in days and there's a really bad smell coming through the letterbox.'

She looked back through the slot. 'And I can hear flies.'

Marshall waited patiently for the SOCO team. She knew Gates would want to be the first into the place.

Fifteen minutes later, the uniforms arrived in a squad car and a couple of PCs helped to keep the more inquisitive neighbours at bay. Technically this wasn't her patch, but no one seemed that interested in jurisdictional boundaries.

Twenty minutes after that, two black vans appeared at the end of the road and the usual dishevelled figure of Gates stepped out of the first.

'Marshall,' he greeted her, placing his case down on the

welcome mat and taking out a pair of latex gloves. 'Do we know who's in there?'

'The ticket office manager from Monument, Graham Parnell.'

Gates's eyes widened. 'Not a coincidence I take it?'

'Unlikely.'

The pathologist knelt down and peered through the letterbox.

'*Lucilia sericata*. Blow fly.'

Marshall looked confused. 'How long do they take to appear.'

'Roughly two weeks, depends if the environment is kept at a nice even temperature.' He closed the letterbox and stood up.

I met him two weeks ago.

'It's going to be quite bad in there, are you sure you want to come in?'

She held up the key.

He was right, the smell of decaying flesh made her gag the moment they stepped inside, even Gates coughed as the miasma hit them.

The flat was a shrine to the seventies. The flock wall-paper and knick-knacks that lined the hall were just as Parnell's mother would have left them. Breathing through her mouth, Marshall followed behind Gates, putting her feet in the same places in the swirling velour carpet.

Passing the kitchen, Marshall noticed a half-eaten meal sitting on the formica table, she thought it was rice until she realised it was moving.

66

GLUE

Flat 37, Ogilvy House, London. Wednesday, December 18. 08:00

The door at the end of the hall was half-closed, Gates took a deep breath and pushed it open.

The flies were everywhere, a black storm circling around the tiny lounge.

It took Marshall a second to recognise the body in the armchair, it was less than human. The upper torso was undressed, skin blackened and putrefying. The head was tipped back and the back half was completely missing.

A shotgun was wedged between his legs, the thumb was still hooked through the trigger guard.

There was a dark spatter pattern across the curtains behind him.

'Suicide?' Gates mumbled, examining the gun.

Marshall didn't hear the rest of what he said. She was staring at what was left of his face.

The man in the chair was not the Parnell she had met at Monument.

She turned to the fake fireplace, scanning along the mantel at the gilt-framed pictures of his mother until she found one of them both.

'How long would you say he's been dead?' she asked, picking up the photo of Parnell and his mum at the beach.

'Two maybe three weeks.'

An icy knot formed in her stomach as she realised it was not Parnell that had turned up at Monument.

'It's not a suicide,' she said under her breath.

'Perhaps not,' said Gates, taking a metal spatula from his case. 'Rigor Mortis should have ended by now. Do you see how he's still clutching the gun?'

He tried to prise the hand away from the weapon but it held fast.

'Looks like the thumb has been superglued to the trigger.'

Marshall felt the world spinning, her palms were clammy, she knew that if she didn't leave soon she would pass out or worse, throw up on the crime scene.

'I just need a minute.'

She went outside and sucked down lungfuls of clean air. The PCs guarding the front door tried not to notice how pale she looked. *I'm not going to throw up*, she told herself closing her eyes and gripping onto the balcony rail until her pulse began to slow.

It might not be him she tried to convince herself, but part of her already knew that it was.

She had met the killer.

67

PUB

Lord Raglan, St Martin's-le-Grand, London. Wednesday, December 18. 14:00

'Jonathan Mayberry has been released without charge,' Donovan said, putting the drinks down on the table.

The pub was half-full, mostly with tourists and far enough away from the station that they were unlikely to bump into anyone they knew.

Marshall took a sip of her wine, it was cold and sharp, and exactly what she needed.

'Did you give the eFit team a description?'

She nodded, still not sure that it would be much help. In hindsight the hair was undoubtedly a wig and the glasses made it virtually impossible to see his real face. But she had, she had stared into the eyes of the killer.

'He's got some balls. I'll give him that.' Donovan raised his pint glass. 'Don't beat yourself up over it.'

'What I can't work out is why. Why take the risk? When he's been so careful to avoid being identified.'

Donovan shrugged. 'Don't try and second guess his motives. He's probably not playing with a full deck. Can you remember what he said exactly? '

She had been over it countless times in her head in the last couple of hours.

'Staff rota, keys, Mayberry,' Marshall counted on her fingers. 'Then he claimed he didn't know it was a murder. Then Salazar called me.'

'Not a lot to go on.'

She took a long sip of her wine, trying to clear the memory of the smell in Parnell's flat. She had to admire Gates's stamina to stay there and process the room, it took less than five minutes before she had to leave.

'Why give us Mayberry?' she asked.

'He's fucking with us. Sending us off on a wild goose chase.'

'I think he wants to get caught. The whole alchemy thing is leading towards something. He's trying to tell us something, but I can't figure out what.'

Donovan shook his head. 'Stick to the facts. This mumbo-jumbo bullshit is just a smoke screen, another diversion. Most people kill other people for very simple reasons: mostly love, hate and money.'

'Other than two of them getting massive payouts five years ago, the victims have no connection. Apart from being murdered by the same guy.'

'Not yet, but it will be there somewhere.'

'You knew Sykes didn't you?'

'Detective Inspector Sykes,' he corrected her. 'Yes, I worked with him at the Met CID, before he went to Special Branch.'

'When was that?'

Donovan's eyes narrowed, glazing over a little. 'Well, that

must have been around the time of the Alice Gross murder. That was 2014.'

'What was he like?'

'Lone wolf. Very private, hardly ever socialised. Rumour was that he had a few sidelines going but nothing was ever proven. He ended up working with the Hong Kong police after he left the spooks.'

'Can you think of any reason why he would end up in a barrel of acid?'

'No, but there will be. These aren't motiveless murders. There'll be something, you just need to go back to the beginning and look again.'

'With Melanie?'

The DCI nodded, downing the rest of his pint. 'Her funeral's tomorrow. I want you down there in case our killer shows up, some of them like to dine out on the grief of others.'

68

FUNERAL

Brookwood Cemetery, Surrey. Thursday, December 19. 09:30

The storm clouds were clearing over the cemetery as the convoy of black cars crawled slowly between the gravestones. Rain had been falling since dawn, dousing the slick granite stones, which were glistening in the rays of the weak winter sun.

A cold layer of mist clung to the long dewy grass. Standing beneath a cluster of old yew trees, Marshall shivered as she waited for the funeral procession to pass into the chapel, their heads bowed respectively. *Should have worn a thicker coat*, she thought, blowing on her hands.

Melanie's body had finally been released by the coroner after Gates had gleaned everything he could. Now it was time for the family to lay her to rest.

Her husband looked terribly frail as the nurse wheeled him into the small church, his thin legs covered by a thick blanket and his head buried beneath a hat and scarf.

There were a few mourners. Marshall counted less than

twenty. Mostly older relatives by the look of them. Marshall spotted Melanie's sister, she could have been her twin, they looked so similar. She was in tears, her husband had his arm around her waist trying to console her or hold her up, she couldn't tell.

No one looked remotely like the man she had thought was Parnell.

Walking up to the chapel, she thought back to the day they buried Will. Then the weather had been beautiful, a bright sunny morning, and she remembered thinking it was just like him to try and brighten up a perfectly miserable day.

The entire college came to pay tribute, which he would have loved. There were so many people, so many flowers and so much pain. She could still see the blame in his parents' eyes as they walked into the church. They all believed it was her fault, her mother had warned her not to go, but she couldn't stay away.

She had to say goodbye.

The night had started just like any other Friday. They met at a pub called the Salamander to take advantage of happy hour; a few of their friends showed up and they all made the most of the cheap drinks. Two hours of tequila slammers and mojitos later, they were ready to move on.

There were certain pubs in Bath that students frequented. Preferring to avoid the sports bars, especially on rugby days, they kept close to Queen Square, catching up with various friends as they moved along John Street.

Will was on fire that night. A dazzling personality at the best of times, he was the life and soul of the party because he was celebrating. The police had offered him a scholarship to study forensics, he was going to get paid to go to university. Will was annoyingly clever, especially in the sciences, but he never bragged about it.

They had met in chemistry and hit it off straight away. She loved the way he would explain things she couldn't understand. He made her laugh out loud when he drew a rude diagram of covalent bonds, causing their teacher to give them both a hard stare. He should have trained to be a doctor, but he wanted to spend his life catching bad guys.

Except that night, outside Moles on George Street, someone took it away.

Marshall had noticed the guy staring at her after a few minutes of being in the bar. It was the kind of attention that you generally ignore and in most cases the bloke normally gets the message pretty quickly.

Except this one didn't.

She had worn a short skirt, the kind that her father would have described as a 'belt'. Will liked her long legs, especially in knee-high boots and she thought he deserved a treat after his hard won scholarship.

'I like your boots,' the neanderthal slurred, coming to stand next to her at the bar.

Will had gone to the toilet. The guy had seen this as an opportunity to chance his luck.

'Thanks,' Marshall replied, trying to be nice.

'Can I buy you a drink?'

'No thanks.'

The guy's eyes were having trouble focusing on her. She could still remember thinking how hammered he was.

'I like your boots,' he repeated, staring at her breasts.

'I know you said.' She turned back to the bar and tried to get the attention of the barman.

'I'm talking to you, bitch. Don't turn away from me.'

He put his hand on her shoulder and spun her around.

'What the fuck!' she shouted into his face, making him step back.

'I just want to buy you a fucking drink,' he complained. 'No need to get all arsey!'

'Just fuck off!' she said, looking around for a bouncer. The bar was heaving and there was no way to see where Will was.

The man disappeared into the throng and two minutes later Will returned, and she told him that she wanted to leave.

This was her first mistake.

The guy and his friends had gone outside for a cigarette and they were there when she and Will came out.

The second mistake was not stopping Will when the dickhead made some snide comment about her arse.

Will was a very fit, six-foot guy with a white-knight complex a mile wide. He detested violence, but he wasn't one to let someone disrespect his girlfriend. Especially when the guy was only just keeping his knuckles off the floor.

The man went down on the first punch and stayed there. She could remember thinking that was the most satisfying thing she had even seen.

Then his friends got involved.

It wasn't a fair fight, not three against one. Will kicked one and managed to wind another with a punch to the stomach, but the last man got his arm around Will's neck.

He couldn't shake him. She remembered the look of

anger on his face as he tried to free himself while the others got slowly to their feet.

They piled into him with feet and fists. She screamed for someone to help but no one came.

Will fell to the floor under the barrage of blows. Marshall tried to help, tearing at the faces with her nails, but they pushed her away.

Then the man was on her, the one from the bar. His hands going up her skirt, grabbing at her knickers. She tried to push him away but he was too strong. She panicked, kicking at him, but he caught her foot and she lost her balance.

The cobblestones were hard and she landed awkwardly. He was on top of her, his weight pressing the breath out of her as he fumbled with his trousers.

She tried to bite him, but he put one arm under her neck making it hard to move her head. She could still smell the sour, beer-soaked breath as he panted over her.

Then Will was on him. Somehow he had managed to get free of the others, he kicked the man hard in the stomach and she felt him roll away.

She remembered how angelic Will looked with the corona of a streetlight behind his head.

As he bent down to help her up, one of them hit him with something heavy. The coroner said it was a loose kerb stone, it crushed the side of his skull.

Her best friend died in her arms.

There were some people that you assume will always be part of your life; ones that you're drawn to, that seem to complete who you are. He had been one of them. When he died, there was a void that nothing seemed to be able to fill.

After the trial, when she had given evidence against all three of them and they had been sent down for fifteen years each, she decided to join the police.

She would become the copper that Will never got to be.

After the service, the mourners trooped back out behind the coffin. The grave was only a short walk from the chapel and Marshall followed them at a respectful distance.

She should have been taking photos, but there was no point. No one looked capable of lifting a chair, let alone a prone sixty-kilo woman.

Once the coffin had been lowered and the liturgies read, she approached the open grave.

'DS Marshall,' the husband greeted her. 'Thank you for coming.'

'My sincere condolences,' she said. 'I'm sorry we haven't found him yet.'

He nodded, his eyes creasing with pain. 'She would have liked you. Melanie was a strong woman too.'

She wanted to ask about what had happened five years ago, but knew that this wasn't the right time. It could wait.

The carer pushed the wheelchair away and Marshall found herself alone by the grave. Taking off her glove, she knelt down and threw some dirt over the coffin. It was a ritual that she had never really understood.

'I'll find him Melanie. I promise,' she whispered under her breath.

69

THERAPY

Queen Victoria Street, London. Thursday, December 19. 14:00

'What is your earliest memory?' the therapist asked with a well-practised smile.

Marshall sat on the sofa, it was uncomfortable and impossible to relax into. Which seemed odd when she considered that was the whole point of the exercise. Doctor Bell had insisted she attend this session as part of her return to work. It was her idea of hell, someone prying around in her subconscious, but she had to do it.

'Drowning.'

The woman's eyes widened a little as she made notes. 'Can you tell me about it.'

Marshall explained how she had been playing with a friend near the Pulteney weir in Bath. The River Avon ran through the middle of the city and a weir was an intriguing place for a seven-year-old. It was summer and the banks of the river were lined with tourists and locals enjoying the warmth of the sun. Her mother had gone to buy them ice-creams leaving strict instructions for the two of them to stay put. Her friend Anj wandered over to the edge of the water the moment Marshall's mother was out of sight. She duly followed and the next thing she could remember was the cold as the water enveloped her.

The flow of the water off the weir pushed her downstream, there were moments of light and dark as she tried to keep her head above water, the few swimming lessons she had were immediately forgotten.

Apparently an off-duty fireman had seen Anj jumping up and down by the water's edge and mistook Marshall's blond hair for a dog. It didn't matter, he still went in after her.

She would never forget the look on her mother's face when she was pulled out onto the riverbank. It was a mixture of disappointment and rage.

'Do you feel as if your mother blamed you for the accident?'

Marshall felt a swell of emotions rising and suppressed them. 'No.'

I don't think she's ever forgiven me.

The woman's eyes narrowed a little. 'Would you say that you have a fear of water?'

'No.'

She made me learn to swim, it was like torture.

'Do you ever wish that you had died that day?'

I wish that they had taken me instead of Will.

'What kind of question is that?'

'It's healthy for us to contemplate our own mortality.'

'Really? I don't see how this is relevant to my returning to work.'

The therapist looked down at her notes. 'It says here that you were involved in a fatal incident recently.'

'I watched two of my team getting blown up.'

'And how did that make you feel?'

Numb.

'What do you mean?'

'Were you scared? Did you feel guilty for surviving?'

'It made me angry.'

'Because you survived?'

'No, because they didn't listen to me. I told them to wait.' There were tears streaming down her cheeks now.

'And they ignored you. Do you blame yourself?'

For so many things.

Marshall could feel the emotions welling up inside her and couldn't hold them back. 'No, I don't, but everyone seems to want to blame me: James blames me for losing the baby. Mum blames me for leaving home, Will's parents for his death. It's like I'm this emotional punchbag for everyone else to offload their shit onto and I hate it. I'm sick of them all telling me how disappointed they are in me. I've done everything I can to do the right thing, to live up to their expectations, and all I get back is criticism. Well, fuck the lot of them.'

She took a deep breath, relaxing her hands where they had gripped the edge of the sofa. Her throat was tight and sore.

The therapist smiled calmly and handed her a Kleenex.

'I think that's enough for our first session.'

70

PULLMAN STILL ALIVE

London. Thursday, December 19. 19:00

Samantha Pullman sat shivering in the darkness. It was the kind of dark where she couldn't tell whether her eyes were open or closed. Only the sound of her own breathing told her she was still alive. Sam had never been so scared.

Her body ached, racked by the uncontrollable shivering that came from withdrawal. She had been through this many times in rehab, but they had soft beds and medicines that brought her down gently.

This was cold-turkey.

The room was freezing and the sheets were damp. Her arms and legs were chained to the bedframe. There was something going into her right arm. She guessed it was some kind of infusion drip.

The man who kidnapped her had left a while ago. Sam assumed he came every day to feed and wash her. There was no dignity left after the second day, her clothes had been spoiled and he changed the sheets without a word.

He was tender when he bathed her. The sponge was warm and smelled of roses. She had begged him to let her go, pleaded and screamed at him, but he said nothing, simply made her comfortable and then left.

By her reckoning this was the twelfth visit, which meant she had been trapped here for nearly two weeks, although it might have been longer. The first few days she was hardly aware of what was going on. The lack of drugs in her system made her weak and delirious. As her mind had cleared she began to focus on the sounds around her. There was a distant thrum of machinery, like being on a ship, and the sounds of rushing water. She wondered if they were on some kind of tanker on its way to a random part of Russia. She knew her father had some powerful enemies, but none of them had ever dared to abduct her before.

There was something strange about the way he treated her. Sam kept replaying the moment in the toilets when he attacked her. How she had fought back, thinking he was trying to rape her.

When Sam woke in the back of his van, she told him she was pregnant. It was an old trick that she used to get herself out of the clutches of over-amorous Russians oligarchs, but in this case it was true.

She was having a baby.

Something changed then, he stopped the van and sat there for the longest time letting the engine idle. Sam could hear him whispering something, like a prayer, over and over again to himself.

Then he injected her with something and she blacked out.

When she woke next she was tied to the bed.
'Help!' she screamed. 'For fuck's sake, anybody!'

71

MEMBERS

Wood Street Station, London. Friday, December 20. 09:00

Biggs re-read the remaining list of names of the Welbeck members. It was slow, but he was making good progress. This was good old-fashioned police work, using the process of elimination. Half of them were scratched out: some were dead, others were overseas. Hours of searching both the police databases and the web had shortened it down to ten names.

The suspects were big players in the city: bankers, hedge fund managers and traders all with public school backgrounds and million plus salaries — an old boy network of the financial elite.

Concentrating on the final ten, he began by looking back over the last five years. He had a theory that whatever triggered the payments to the first two victims had happened five years ago.

'DNA has come back with a match on the body from the river,' Baxter interrupted, dropping a report onto his desk.

Biggs picked up the folder and opened it.

'Gillian MacIntyre?'

'Arrested for drunk driving five years ago. Car was a mess. She'd stacked it into a lamp post just the other side of Southwark Bridge.'

'Five years ago?'

'Interesting coincidence,' Baxter said, raising his wiry old eyebrows.

'No such thing,' Biggs replied, then looking back at his laptop. 'There's a MacIntyre on this list. William MacIntyre, he's a portfolio manager at Citadel Investment.'

Baxter leaned in to look at the list. Biggs caught a whiff of Menthol and Camphor — Vicks Vaporub.

'Has anyone reported her missing?' Biggs asked, trying not to get too excited.

Baxter stepped back. 'I'll go and check.'

'Have you seen Marshall?' Biggs took out his phone.

'Said something about going to see her father.'

72

HOSPITAL

West Middlesex Hospital. Friday, December 20. 10:00

Her father's blue eyes looked straight through her when she arrived. There was no hint of recognition. As Marshall came onto the ward, the nurse warned her that he had suffered a series of vascular strokes overnight, robbing him of what little memory he had left.

Beside his bed, her mother sat stoically holding his hand. Her eyes were filled with grief, as if he had already gone. It was the unspoken wish between them. A guilty thought that neither were brave enough to share. That he would pass and that their suffering would be over. People would say that it was a kindness or a blessed relief. It felt wrong to want it, but there was hardly anything left of the man she loved, and Marshall knew that this wasn't how he would want to be remembered.

'Hi Mum,' she whispered, kissing her on the cheek. 'How's he been?'

'The doctors said I should prepare for the worst,' she said, her voice was thin and tight from crying.

Marshall hugged her, feeling the sobs run through her body as her mother held her tightly.

She wanted to say it would be okay, that everything was going to be all right, but it wouldn't. This was the end and there was no way to sugar-coat it.

'He's had a good life,' her mum reflected, dabbing at her cheeks with a tissue. 'I don't want him to suffer any more.'

'No,' Marshall agreed, looking at her father who seemed to have fallen asleep. He had always been such a strong, healthy man, out in all weathers tending to his vegetables or hanging off a ladder picking plums and pears. *He wouldn't want us moping around*, she thought, sitting on the bed and taking his hand in hers. 'Do you remember that time I broke the car window?'

Her mum laughed. 'He was so angry. He loved that car. I should never have let you play in there.'

'Not with a spanner.'

The light came back into her mother's eyes. 'And the time you painted half the shed silver with that spray can?'

It was Marshall's turn to laugh. 'I hated pink.'

'He brought that bike all the way home on the train.'

She could still remember the day he taught her to ride. Holding the saddle and running behind her as she wobbled down their street. It had tassels and things in the spokes that made a clacking noise. She loved everything about it except the colour, so she sprayed it silver with a can she found in the shed, the inside of the door still had the outline of a bike picked out in a silver cloud.

'His bloody sheds,' her mother said with a sigh.

'We'll sort it together. I'm sure Uncle George will help.'

They sat watching him sleep for a while. Listening to the

sound of his breathing, wondering if it was going to be his final one. Suddenly, he opened his eyes and there was the smile. 'Hello love, nice to see you.'

'Hi Dad.'

73

FIFTH VICTIM

Deutsche Bank, London. Friday, December 20. 13:00

William MacIntyre had just closed the biggest deal of his career. He looked out over the city feeling like the 'King of the World'. This was the one that would secure his bonus and kick start his own fund.

The desk phone rang, breaking him out of his reverie.

'Your car is waiting sir,' his assistant's voice said through the speaker.

'Tell him I'll be down in five.'

He ended the call and sat down behind his desk.

Opening a web browser, he logged into his online bank and checked his balance. There was close to fifty-million dollars split between the two Swiss accounts. Neither of which had been disclosed during the divorce. With the bonus from this deal it was going to be close to sixty by the weekend. It had taken years to get his life back on track; she had taken his kids, his house and cost him his job.

Now he was a free man with enough equity to start his

own company. The resignation email was sitting in draft waiting to be sent.

King of the World, he thought, closing down the browser and opening the email.

Clicking send made every minute of the last five years worth it.

Stepping into the lift, his phone vibrated. Assuming it was a reply to his resignation, MacIntyre took it out eagerly. There was a message from Sykes sitting in his private email.

He waited until the doors closed and opened the message.

The subject line simply read: 'Samantha.'

MacIntyre hadn't heard from the ex-detective since he had left for Hong Kong. His thumb instinctively went to the delete icon. He wished he had never met Sam Pullman. She was toxic, like a virus, corrupting everything and everyone she touched. Sykes had got him out of trouble before and he wouldn't have contacted him unless it was important.

He scrolled down to the body of the message.

Sam's disappeared and the others are dead. I think someone's following me.

The words were made all the more sinister by the fact that Sykes didn't answer his phone when MacIntyre tried to call him.

The parking garage was a concrete bunker two floors beneath the office. Use of the company cars was a privilege that only the partners and senior VPs were afforded. They were badges of status; Rolls Royces and Daimlers lined one side of the underground car park, each one with a personalised number plate.

The parking attendant was nowhere to be seen, but MacInytre noticed that one of the Bentleys was idling and made his way towards it.

Sliding into the back seat of the car, he caught the reflection of his driver in the rear view mirror. It wasn't one of the usual guys, but he didn't care, he was too distracted by the message from Sykes. He should have known better than to contact him directly, it was a breach of their agreement.

'Where to sir?'

MacIntyre looked up from his phone. 'Didn't Shelley tell you?' he snapped. His assistant was usually more organised than this.

'No.'

'The Connaught.'

74

SUSPECT

Wood Street Station, London. Friday, December 20. 16:00

Her mother hadn't wanted her to go. There was a chance her father wouldn't make it through the next twenty-four hours, but Marshall couldn't just sit there and make idle conversation. It was painful enough listening to his laboured breathing, let alone witness the emotional trauma that her mother was going through.

She made her excuses, promising her mum she would come back later.

It was one of the hardest goodbyes she had made since holding Will in her arms. Kissing the top of her father's bald head, she let her lips linger, breathing him in, he still smelled like dad.

She smoothed down the wayward wisps of grey-white hair and stroked the salt-and-pepper beard.

'Bye Dad.'

His eyes opened, there was nothing but a vacant gaze staring back at her.

. . .

Biggs sprang up from his chair like an over-excited puppy when Marshall walked into the office.

She was exhausted. The morning had been an emotional roller-coaster and the message from Biggs had been a welcome distraction.

'What've you got then?'

He handed her the list of names from the Welbeck, one of them was heavily underlined. 'William MacIntyre.'

'Forensics got a match on the body from the river. It's his wife.' He handed her a photo of a forty-year-old man in a smart dark suit standing next to a beautiful blonde woman at a function. It took Marshall a second to recognise Samantha Pullman.

'He knew her?'

Biggs grinned. 'I think we have ourselves a suspect.'

Marshall didn't look convinced. 'You think he murdered his wife?'

'They divorced five years ago.'

'Because of Samantha?'

He took out a record of their divorce. 'They filed under unreasonable behaviour.'

She took the print out and read through the notes. 'Everything's pointing to the same year. We need to find out what happened back then. Have you found any connection to the others?'

'Not yet,' Biggs said, his smile fading.

'Right, let's go and get MacIntyre, he'll have to ID the body.'

Donovan appeared from his office, his face was flushed as he struggled to put on his jacket.

'Whatever you lot are gabbling on about can wait. We've

got a major incident down near St. Paul's. Counter-terror reports a Bentley's been parked up in front of the cathedral. The driver's got a bomb strapped to his chest.'

75

ST PAUL'S

St Paul's Cathedral, London. Friday, December 20. 17:00

The streets around the cathedral were cordoned off, bringing the rush hour traffic to a standstill. There were uniformed officers blocking access on all roads when Marshall, Salazar and Donovan arrived. Donovan and the acting DI made their way over to the command vehicle; a long white lorry parked on Cannon Street.

Marshall went over to the cordon.

A helicopter hovered in the darkening sky, training its spotlight on the Bentley. It was parked outside the southern entrance to the cathedral. The bomb squad robot was tracking slowly towards the car, with a camera mounted on its extendable arm. Masked counter terrorism officers were patrolling the perimeter, all carrying SIG MCX carbines.

Marshall could just make out the man in the driver's seat. He was shaking his head as the machine drove towards him.

'Marshall!' Donovan shouted from the command centre. 'You need to see this.'

The control vehicle was packed with surveillance systems and operators. Radio chatter was streaming over the speakers and screens showed images from all aspects of the cathedral and the car.

One of the monitors was patched into the feed from the remote camera on the robot.

As the image stabilised she recognised the face of MacIntyre, his mouth taped shut with duct tape. His eyes were wild and he was sweating profusely.

'William MacIntyre,' Marshall said. 'He's the Alchemist.'

Donovan looked confused. 'When exactly were you going to tell me?'

'I've only just found out myself.'

The operator angled the camera down through the window.

His hands were taped to the steering wheel and there was a large black square strapped over his Saville Row suit. There were a series of symbols painted onto the plastic casing and a digital timer.

It read 0:29:01:15.

They watched in silence as the seconds drained away.

'Less than half an hour,' Donovan said with a sigh. 'Marshall do you know what those symbols mean?'

She didn't.

Salazar came back from talking to the Incident Commander. 'Bomb squad are prepping to go in.'

'Not sure if that's a good idea,' Marshall warned, remembering what happened at Harbour Quay.

'These are specialists,' Salazar said, her face trying hard not to sneer and failing.

Marshall took a photo of the symbols and tried to send them to the professor.

'Mobile networks are locked down,' Donovan said, handing her a radio. 'They don't want any chance of a remote detonation.'

'I need to get a message to Professor Gresham.'

Salazar glared at her, as if to remind her of their last conversation.

'Send a bike,' Donovan suggested.

Marshall ran outside and went over to one of the traffic cops that was helping to deal with the chaos caused by the roadblock.

'Hi, can I borrow your bike?'

His reaction was one of confusion and amusement, as if to say: 'You're joking?'

She flashed her warrant card and he shrugged, handing her the keys.

The BMW R1200RT was parked with four others on the side of the road. Marshall grabbed the helmet that was sitting on the seat and tried it on. It was too big, and fell in front of her eyes. She left it on the saddle of one of the others and simply tied her hair back.

The bike felt heavy as she pushed it off the stand. All of the traffic guys were watching her and she wasn't about to give them the satisfaction of falling off.

Marshall loved bikes, especially big ones. Will had a Honda Fireblade and she'd made him teach her how to ride it on their second date.

She revved the engine, feeling the power between her

legs and hit the siren. If she was going to get there fast she was going to need to break a few traffic laws.

She wove between the stationary traffic on Fleet Street, making her way west towards King's College. Black cabs and Routemaster buses were gridlocked all the way back to the Strand. She accelerated between the corridor of vehicles hardly slowing at red lights until she reached Arundel Street. Cutting across the traffic she went left and down towards the river.

The sound of the engine echoed along the narrow alley of Strand Lane, reaching the entrance to the College she left the bike and ran up the stone stairs. Gresham was in the middle of a special Christmas Lecture for the Antiquarian Society, the receptionist informed her. Marshall ignored her and made for the theatre.

'This depiction of hell engraved during the thirteenth century was typical of the age. In contrast to the light and orderly images of heaven,' Gresham's voice intoned as she entered.

The lecture theatre was dark, an image of a demon feeding bodies into a fire was projected onto the large screen.

She didn't have time to wait for him to finish.

'Professor Gresham?' Marshall shouted, walking towards the front of the theatre, the eyes of his students following her.

He looked confused. 'DS Marshall, this is unexpected.'

'I need you to look at this.'

He was about to protest when she handed him her phone. The image of the serpent eating its tail stopped him.

'It's the Ouroboros. The final transformation.'

'It's painted onto a bomb. Is this part of his journey?'

He nodded his head. 'Indeed, the last part of his great work. Turning base metals into precious ones. This is the symbol for Chrysopoeia, the transmutation of gold.'

He turned to a member of the audience. 'Professor Davies, would you kindly remind us of the phrase associated with the Ouroboros?'

'The all is one,' replied the older man proudly.

He gave her back the phone. 'The all is one. That the first day should make the last.'

Marshall's radio squawked.

It was Donovan. 'Marshall, where the fuck are you? They're about to try and disarm the fucking bomb.'

'I'm with Gresham. I think it's the real thing, the serpent is a symbol of rebirth.'

The professor nodded, impressed with her interpretation.

'Get your arse back here now, and bring Doctor Dolittle with you.'

76

GOLD

St Paul's Cathedral, London. Friday, December 20. 18:00

Gresham looked anxious when they got back to the bike. Since neither of them had helmets she drove more carefully back to St Paul's. He put his arms around her waist, pressing their bodies close together. Marshall could feel him against her back. His grip tightened as she took the bends. It was a distraction she didn't need right now, but it was a nice one.

Donovan was waiting by the truck when they arrived.

'Five minutes left,' he said, showing her the feed on a tablet.

The bomb squad had taken the door off the Bentley and two technicians in heavy body armour were kneeling behind shields next to the car.

One of them leaned in with a pair of wire cutters and forced them between the straps of the bomb.

The professor seemed less interested in the screen, he was looking around them, like a tourist.

'Why here?' he muttered to himself.

'Maximum disruption,' Marshall replied. 'Half of the city has ground to a standstill. If the bomb was large enough it could take out most of the financial district.'

'No, the people and places he has chosen so far have had meaning.'

Marshall nodded at St Paul's. 'Doesn't that count.'

'St Paul's was destroyed in the Great Fire. It doesn't follow the pattern they've all been underground or underwater.'

'First strap removed,' came the voice of the army officer.

Marshall looked at the video stream, watching the time running down. There were less than two minutes remaining.

'Can you think of any other reason for him to be left here?' she asked.

Frowning, the professor folded his arms and looked down at the ground. 'It has extensive crypts, perhaps there's something buried below us that may have some bearing, but I'm not a tour guide.'

'Second strap cut, wait —.'

There was a tense silence as everyone held their breath listening to the static hiss from the radio.

'Sixty seconds,' warned one of the team.

'Nearly there.'

The second strap came away leaving one more. On the screen Marshall could see a dark stain spreading across MacIntyre's trousers, his legs were shaking uncontrollably.

'Forty seconds.'

The cutters went under the third strap. Marshall couldn't help but admire how calm the officer's voice sounded and how steady his hand was.

As the blades sliced through the fabric she saw the

hidden wire, but it was too late, there was a flash of light and the screen went dark.

They all ducked instinctively as the bomb detonated.

The Bentley bucked and the windscreen shattered, smoke billowing from the driver's seat. Marshall ran with the others towards the car. The bomb disposal team were laying on the ground, their armoured suits peppered with tiny holes. The fire teams were already dowsing the car with hoses.

MacIntyre was still sitting in the seat, his body glinting in the beams of their torches.

'What is that?' Marshall asked, looking around at the firemen.

The ambulance crew arrived and tended to the two specialists.

She picked up one of their discarded shields. It had protected them from the worst of the shrapnel.

Holding it up to the helicopter's spotlight, Marshall saw tiny golden drops embedded in the molten holes of the perspex.

'Metal,' she said, looking at the body of MacIntyre. 'He's been shot with what looks like gold.'

77

DEBRIEF

Wood Street Station, London. Friday, December 20. 21:00

'So your alchemist is dead,' Salazar began, looking directly at Marshall without blinking. 'Which leaves us with an interesting problem. Who the fuck is the killer?'

Marshall could hear the desperation in her voice, this was a woman watching her career prospects evaporating before her eyes.

'No one? Do we have anything?' she appealed to the room.

The team stared back at her blankly.

'Biggs what did we get from CCTV?'

Biggs cleared his throat and walked over to the plasma screen. 'A camera on the east side captured the driver getting out at five o'clock.' He tapped on the screen and a video showed a man getting out of the Bentley wearing a chauffeur's uniform including a cap and dark glasses. Biggs switched the feed and they watched him walk straight into the church. 'He never came back out.'

'So what is he? A fucking ghost?' asked Devlin.

'He got changed and left by another exit,' Marshall suggested.

Salazar paused the playback. 'Go through all the footage on males exiting the church after five. Use what we know about his approximate height and weight. Devlin where are we with follow-up on MacIntyre?'

Devlin came over to the screen and pulled up pictures of the victim and his wife.

'Portfolio manager, worked at Citadel Investment for the last five years, before that was at Goldman Sachs. Got divorced around the same time as the career change. Three kids, all at private boarding schools. No previous, although she was done for totalling their car.'

'When?' Donovan asked, coming out of his office. Marshall noted that his shirt sleeves were rolled up, a sure sign that they weren't going home any time soon.

Devlin looked back through his notes. 'Six years ago.'

'When exactly?' Marshall asked.

'Twenty-third of December, 2014,' Devlin replied.

'I take it you have a theory Marshall?' Donovan asked, before Salazar had a chance to shut her down.

Marshall stood up and went to the whiteboard. Picking up a marker pen, she wrote the names of the first two victims. 'The payments to Gladwell and Reynolds were early in January 2015. MacIntyre was a wealthy man who knew the Pullmans.' She added the MacIntyres and Samantha Pullman to her diagram and drew lines between them. 'So, what if they were all involved in something that happened around that time?'

Salazar intervened. 'But they don't know each other.'

'Look at who we've got so far.' She added the symbols under each name as she called them out. 'A wife cheating on her sick husband. A hacker. A wealthy banker. His ex-wife with a drinking problem. A party girl.' She added Sykes to the list. 'And a bent copper.'

They all looked at her blankly.

In the centre of the ring of names she wrote: "Lord Pullman".

'And a very rich daddy. Who paid off Melanie, Reynolds, and I bet if you dig around you'll find Sykes as well.'

'What for?' Donovan asked.

Marshall tapped on the symbols. 'Magic.'

'What the fuck are you talking about?' Salazar interrupted.

'To make something disappear.'

78

SAM

London. Saturday, December 21. 08:00

'How long are you going to keep me here?' Samantha asked, while the man retied the blindfold.

'Is this the child of the Alchemist?' His mouth was close to her ear, the voice deep and husky.

'What?'

'William MacIntyre. Are you carrying his child?' There was a strange lilt, like the hint of an accent, but she couldn't place it.

'It's none of your business.'

'Oh, but it is.'

79

SEASIDE

Wood Street Station, London. Saturday, December 21. 09:00

'It's your father,' the voicemail began. Marshall closed her eyes, with everything else that was going on, she hadn't wanted to think about it.

Her mother continued. 'The doctor says he passed away in his sleep.'

She squeezed her eyes with her fingers, failing to stop the tears from coming. Trying to console herself with the idea that he had left his body weeks ago, that this was just what had been left behind.

Come on Pip, don't let the seagulls eat your ice cream.

She called her mother.

'Sorry mum. I should have been there. I'll come over and get you.'

'It's fine, Uncle George said he'd come and take me home.'

'Okay, I'll come over later.'

Her mother ended the call. There was nothing else to

say. The word 'fine' cut Marshall like a knife. It meant everything but fine, it was laden with so many other underlying connotations. She had the right to be angry with her daughter, who had been too scared to stay and witness her father's death.

Uncle George was her father's older brother. He was a London cabbie and usually had an interesting story about some celebrity or other he had picked up in his taxi. Marshall had always liked him, he looked a lot like her dad, but with a darker sense of humour.

He would look after her mother for now.

'Fuck!' she screamed at the toilet door.

Life had an annoying habit of doing the exact opposite of what she needed it to. Somehow Marshall had to try and function, to ignore the yawning chasm of guilt and sadness that opened up inside her.

It was the same feeling after Will. The need to curl up and die, to crawl into a dark place and cease to exist, anything but have to bear the pain of loss.

After Will's funeral, it had taken weeks before she felt like facing the world. Her dad had been the one that had finally persuaded her to go out. He could always get under her defences, even as a stroppy teenager he could make her smile.

He brought her beans on toast — her favourite meal and probably the only thing he knew how to make. She could still picture him in her mother's apron standing at the open door to her bedroom with a tray and a steaming mug of tea.

'Let's go to the seaside,' he suggested while she wolfed down the meal. The beans had to be covered in cheese and brown sauce, just the way she liked them. Will always said it was a crime to mix sauces, but she didn't care.

He drove them to Weston-super-Mare.

When she was younger they used to go there every summer. She adored the pier and the arcades, the hot chips and the ice cream. It was everything you could ever want when you were seven. Long, hot summer days that never seemed to end.

It took over an hour to get there and it rained all the way. They listened to one of his Smiths CDs and laughed about how miserable they were going to be when they got there.

The sun made a fleeting appearance when they reached the pier and he bought her a ninety-nine and a large pot of two-pence coins so they could spend the afternoon on the penny falls.

It was a good day, one that she would remember forever. That was what he did best: no judgement, no questions just being there and showing her there were still good times to be had.

Tears streamed down her face, and she laughed at herself. Sitting in the stalls of the station toilet weeping like a seven-year-old.

She pulled off a length of toilet roll and dried her eyes, remembering what her dad had said that day.

'Pull yourself together Pip,' she said to herself. 'Before the seagulls eat your ice cream.'

80

FINDING

Wood Street Station, London. Saturday, December 21. 10:00

Biggs was halfway through a slice of cold pizza when Marshall returned to her desk. Donovan had bought them for the team yesterday evening and they had pulled an all-nighter going through incidents from the end of 2014.

'You all right?' he asked, noting her red, puffy eyes.

'Fine,' she said, picking out a slice. 'You found anything useful?'

'Loads. Where do you want to start?'

'The night that MacIntyre's wife crashed the car.'

Biggs tapped his laptop and logged back into HOLMES. The list of reported crimes scrolled down off the screen.

'They're mostly shoplifting, moped muggings and disorderly conduct,' he said, flicking through the list.

'Narrow the search down, just the most serious ones.'

He changed the parameters and the list reduced dramatically.

There were now a list of about ten open cases, five of which were assaults and the others were a mixture of theft and credit card fraud.

Except one.

'What's that?' she asked, squinting at his screen.

'Hit and run.' He clicked on the link and opened the report. 'Elizabeth Fabell, an accountant at KPMG, struck down by a car on the night of the twenty-third.'

'She died?'

'No, the medics managed to revive her, she was taken to St Thomas's in a coma. No witnesses or CCTV.'

'Who was the investigating officer?'

He scrolled down to the end of the report. 'Fuck, it was Sykes.'

'Pull up all of the files on her.'

He scrolled back up to the top of the page. 'There aren't any.'

'What do you mean there aren't any?'

'It's got a case number, but there's no evidence log, no witness statements of any kind. Nothing.'

'Do me a favour and check who charged MacIntyre's wife on the night of the accident,' she said, tapping the case number into her phone before heading down the three flights of stairs to the basement.

Although the HOLMES system had been running for nearly twenty years, it was still police procedure to keep paper copies of everything. The files were kept in the archives, which were held in secure storage after a case was closed. Unsolved and open cases were kept onsite for faster access.

Since the electronic version of the case system was named 'Holmes', the curator was commonly referred to as

'Watson'. She was a grey-haired woman, whose real name was Bellamy. She had a sharp tongue, and the temperament of a mother superior who treated the records like her religion. It was a sedentary job that pulled full salary and was thought by most as an easy way to bide your time until the pension kicked in.

'Detective Sergeant Marshall,' she said, folding up her newspaper like an old shopkeeper. 'How may I help you?'

'I'm looking for the files on this case.' Marshall wrote down the case number on a slip of paper.

Bellamy took it and turned to the long shelves of storage behind her.

'Give me five minutes.'

The wait was the longest five minutes Marshall had ever endured. She paced around the waiting area. Patience was not one of her better qualities. Her father used to call her the 'five-minute-wonder' because she would lose interest in anything that took longer.

Bellamy's face was a mixture of confusion and dismay when she returned, it told Marshall everything she needed to know.

'I'm afraid the case files were removed four years ago,' she said, showing Marshall a removal slip. 'By a Detective Inspector Sykes.'

'Come in,' Donovan said before Marshall could knock on his door.

'It's about DI Sykes, sir.'

Donovan rubbed his chin, feeling the two-day stubble. 'You've found something?'

He rummaged around in his drawer and pulled out an

old electric shaver, tried to switch it on and realised the batteries were dead.

'There was an incident around the time of Mrs MacIntyre's crash. Sykes was the SIO on both cases, but all of the files are missing on HOLMES.'

He shrugged. 'Have you tried the archives? This wouldn't be the first time the system has screwed up.'

'I've already been to see Watson. Sykes pulled the files four years ago.'

'What was the incident?'

'Hit and run. A woman by the name of Elizabeth Fabell. She was rushed to St Thomas's. Biggs is getting her records sent over.'

'And Sykes was involved in both?'

'Don't you think it's a bit coincidental that MacIntyre's wife has a crash on the same night?'

'Not necessarily, if he was the most senior officer on duty.'

'But why would CID get involved in a traffic accident?'

Donovan shrugged.

81

THE HOUSE

Wood Street Station, London. Sunday, December 22. 00:01

The records showed that the Fabells lived in a detached house in a leafy suburb of Surrey.

Marshall had long since stopped being surprised by the normality of the life that a killer could maintain. The media created monsters out of them, but these were people you could pass in the street and never know what they were capable of. It was so easy to forget that they had mothers, partners and even children. That they bought their groceries from Tesco, listened to iTunes or watched movies at the weekend.

They were psychopaths, able to disassociate their terrible actions from their normal life. It was this personality trait that made them so fascinating to crime novelists and readers alike. To be so devious, to be able to lead two completely separate lives without any remorse.

. . .

Marshall waited in the van at the end of their street, watching the firearms team taking position around the house on one of the video feeds.

It was dark, the streetlights had switched off at eleven, leaving the lights of the house as the only source of illumination.

The images from their body cameras showed a well-tended garden and a pretty, gabled house.

The ground floor rooms were dark, but two of the bedrooms were still lit. There was no sign of movement and the chatter on the radios was guarded. The explosion at St Paul's had heightened their awareness, everyone was on the lookout for booby traps and IEDs.

'Red one in position,' reported the first team at the rear of the property.

'Copy that,' said the commander from the front of the van.

Biggs discovered that Elizabeth Fabell survived the hit and run, but never regained consciousness. Her husband, Alexander, was a research chemist at a global pharmaceutical company with a long history of psychological problems. He left his job to take care of her after there was nothing else the hospital could offer.

She died four years later. Marshall couldn't imagine what it must have been like for him to watch her wither away. It was hard enough over this last year with her dad. Four years of mental torture could twist a man's mind in all sorts of ways.

. . .

'Red two moving towards the entrance, no sign of activity,' a second voice reported.

'Proceed with extreme caution.'

'Copy that.'

Searching Sykes's apartment had come up with nothing. They were hoping to find some of the missing files from her accident. Retiring detectives often took their work home; unable to admit defeat on the cases they never solved. Stranger killings were like crossword puzzles without any clues. There was something about the mental challenge that was addictive — the kind of problem that would haunt you in the still hours before dawn. It became obsessive, especially on long running cases, it broke people, the thought of not knowing, of not having closure.

Unfortunately, Sykes wasn't that kind of guy. His flat looked as if he had never lived there, if he had kept anything it was in some garage somewhere that no one would find.

His records were mostly redacted after he moved to Special Branch. When he left the force he moved in even darker circles.

All they knew was that he lived alone and travelled widely. There was an ex-wife, who had no interest in discussing him. The man was a ghost, no one would mourn his passing.

'Red two entering the premises.'

Marshall held her breath, unconsciously counting down from ten while she waited for the explosion, but none came.

'Clear.'

The next few seconds were a blur of movement. Once

inside the house, the team moved quickly from one room to the next, the laser sights on their weapons sweeping through the darkened rooms.

From the video feed Marshall could see the inside of the house was a mess. Like a hoarder's den it was full of rubbish: notes and papers covered the walls and there were books scattered everywhere.

At the back they discovered a room with a hospital bed and monitoring equipment. It was nowhere near as hi-tech as the system that Melanie Gladwell had bought for her husband, it looked second-hand, like old NHS equipment from the seventies.

'Red two check the bedrooms,' ordered the commander.

'Roger that.'

The camera feed showed the men climbing the stairs, navigating the stacks of books that were left in random piles on the steps.

Each of the bedrooms were searched thoroughly. Two of them were used for storage, filled with boxes of medical supplies.

The third room was decorated as a nursery. There was a child's cot with a mobile hanging silently above it. Prints of unicorns and fairies decorated the walls and everything was covered in a thick layer of dust. No one had entered the room for years.

She was pregnant, Marshall thought to herself.

'House is clear,' said the leader of red one.

It was two o'clock in the morning before forensics arrived.

The crime scene officer looked as if someone had dragged him out of bed.

Marshall was studying the walls around the old hospital bed when the pathologist found her. There were hundreds of drawings pinned haphazardly over every available inch of space. Reading some of the notes scrawled on them, it was obviously the work of a deranged mind. Diagrams of the body from ancient Chinese acupuncture texts were pasted next to old medieval woodcuts of trepanning. Illustrations showed demons being released from holes bored into the skull of the unfortunate patient.

The research of a desperate man, Marshall thought, *one looking for a cure.* She tried to imagine what it must have been like to be trapped in this house for years. Whatever his previous mental issues had been, he had clearly lost his mind trying to find a way to bring her back.

'He was a chemist?' the SOCO asked, opening his bag and handing her a pair of latex gloves.

'Research chemist for GSK,' she answered without taking her eyes from the notes. 'He was trying to save her.'

'And she died?'

'Six weeks ago.'

Other members of the forensics team walked into the room.

'Start over here,' the SOCO said, walking over to the bed.

'He sat and watched her for four years,' Marshall said, pulling on the gloves and picking up a journal that sat on a bedside cabinet. The pages were filled with times and dates, doses and readings. 'He kept her alive all that time.'

The photographer began to take shots of the walls. The flash was blinding in the dim light of the room.

Marshall walked out into the hallway and left them to their work.

. . .

Donovan was waiting outside with Salazar.

The street was lit up by police cars and support vehicles. The neighbours watched wide-eyed from their bedroom windows.

'Anything useful?' The DCI asked.

'It's definitely him.'

'So where is he now?'

82

SUNDAY

Chiswick. Sunday, December 22. 12:01

The house was quiet.

Marshall let herself in and took off her shoes in case her mother was sleeping.

She stood in the hallway listening for any sign of movement. It was a strange sensation being in her parents' house waiting for someone to come and greet her. Although it had never been her home, she had come to think of it as where they belonged. There was so much of her father here, his essence was imprinted in every corner of every room. From the photos and mementoes of their lives that lined the shelves, to the small unconscious things: the angle of a chair where he used to sit looking out into the garden, the position of a light in the lounge — tiny details that made it his house.

Except he wasn't there any more. He was nothing more than a memory now, a shadow that flickered in her mind like an old home movie.

'Hello love,' her mother said, coming down the stairs.

She was still in her dressing gown. Her hair unbrushed and her make-up smudged into dark circles around her eyes.

'Mum.' Marshall gathered her up in her arms and hugged her tightly.

They went into the kitchen and Marshall made them a pot of tea. She only drank it at her mother's, like some kind of weird Japanese ceremony, every conversation always began with the making of the tea.

'I know it was hard for you,' her mother began, 'to see your father like that. He wouldn't have wanted you to be upset.'

Marshall had a hundred reasons why she couldn't be there, but none of them mattered. The truth was she didn't want to watch him die. It was too hard, too painful and her mother knew it.

'When he was still himself, he used to talk about how proud he was of your courage. That you went out every day into a world of violence and corruption, and faced it. I've never understood why you wanted to do those things. Even after Will. I wanted you to be safe, to keep you out of harm's way. That's what mothers do I suppose.'

'But I couldn't save him!' Marshall said, feeling the tears rolling down her cheeks.

'That wasn't your fault. You can't spend the rest of your life trying to undo the past. When we moved here your father called it a new chapter, and it was. We were happy, we had each other. You need to find that too.'

'I thought I had, once.'

Her mother put her hand tenderly on her cheek. 'Will wouldn't have wanted you to waste your life trying to find forgiveness. You're the only one who can change that. Don't spend your life regretting things. You're too much like your father, you bury your feelings too deeply.'

She sighed. 'He left something for you. Made me promise to give it to you when he died.'

Getting to her feet, her mother went over to one of the kitchen cupboards and took out an old biscuit tin.

'I've never looked in it,' she said, handing it to her.

The tin was heavy and Marshall could feel something sliding about inside. It took a few attempts to get the lid off.

There were hundreds of photographs inside. Everyone of them a memory from her childhood and a short hand-written note.

'Remember the seagulls.'

83

MAPS

King's College, London. Monday, December 23. 10:00

Gresham was drinking coffee in the refectory with two other members of staff. The canteen was virtually empty, Marshall assumed because most of the students had gone home for Christmas. She wondered why he was still working, but thought better than to pry into his personal life.

The professor spotted Marshall as she walked in and came over to meet her.

'Have you found him?' He looked concerned, his dark brown eyes staring into hers.

'No. Is there somewhere we can talk?'

She could see his students glancing over to them, gossiping about the two of them.

'Of course. I need to take this back to the library anyway.' He held up a worn leather book.

. . .

Walking along the corridor, she told him about Elizabeth Fabell, her accident and what they had found in the house.

'Have you found any connections to the other victims?'

'Only to Sykes — he was the investigating officer on both her accident and Mrs MacIntyre's crash.'

'You think MacIntyre's wife struck her with the car?'

Marshall nodded. 'And Sykes was paid to cover it up.'

'Why?'

She shrugged. 'I don't know yet. But Fabell's had years to plan this, there's got to be something that connects them.'

'All things are connected.' Gresham said, reaching the doors to the library. 'What did you want to ask me?'

Marshall looked out of one of the windows down onto the quad. The glass was frosted with ice and the students were bundled up in winter coats and scarves. 'Today's the anniversary of his wife's accident. I think he's working up to something, but we have no idea where he is.'

'And you think he still has Samantha Pullman?'

'Yes.'

'Come with me.'

They entered the stillness of the reading room of the Maughan Library. It was a circular space with bookshelves that rose up the walls on three levels towards a domed glass ceiling. A few students were busy studying at the desks, their laptops surrounded by old textbooks. It was the most serene place Marshall had ever experienced.

She followed Gresham up a metal staircase to the second level. He would stop every so often and take out a book, consulting the indexes before handing some of them to her.

After thirty minutes, she was beginning to lose her patience. 'What are we doing?' she whispered.

He glared at her, raising one finger to his lips.

They came to a door with 'Foyle's Special Collection' written in gold lettering above it. He ran his security pass through the door lock and it opened.

The lights flickered on as they entered, the room was cool and there were no windows. There were wooden plan chests along two walls and a large flat table in the centre.

'At first I thought your killer was using the locations of buildings that have survived the Great Fire.'

He put on a pair of white cotton gloves and went over to one of the drawers. Pulling out a large sheet of paper, he carefully laid it out on the table.

'You can put the books down,' he said, motioning for her to place them on the side.

The map was an old print of London, the date was 1666.

'The Great Fire of 1666 laid waste five-sixths of the walled medieval city,' he explained, pointing at various parts on the map. 'From Fleet Street in the west to the Tower of London in the east, and north from the bank of the Thames to the wall at Cripplegate. In many places the ground was too hot to walk on for several days afterwards.'

'And the church we found Melanie in survived?'

'Yes, St Andrew Undershaft was one of a handful that did. When your second victim was found at Monument I thought that was leading towards a pattern. I was wrong.'

'We found old maps at his house.'

Gresham picked up one of the books. It was a London guide from the 1930s, he opened it at an early map of the tube system.

'Four of his victims were found within the City, and most within easy access of an underground station.' He picked up a few of the small lead counters that were used to hold down the edges of the map and placed them over specific spots on the map. 'Monument, St Paul's, Temple, London Bridge.'

'But not Leadenhall or Harbour Quay.'

He shook his head, placing a lead counter in the docklands. 'He didn't leave a body at Harbour Quay, and as for St Andrew Undershaft.'

'He used an underground car park.'

Gresham pulled out another map from a drawer and laid it on the table next to the first.

'This was Bazalgette's plans for the sewerage system. By 1875, he'd built over eighty-two miles of sewers under London. A network of interconnecting, brick-lined tunnels that connected to six larger, intercepting sewers. I now believe your killer has been moving through the subterranean foundations of London.'

'That doesn't explain why he left them in those specific locations.'

Gresham scratched his beard. 'The outlier is the Harbour Quay incident. Something changed his mind. He took her outside of the city.'

'I think she's pregnant.'

'Why would that make a difference?'

'Because his wife was expecting when she got knocked down and Fabell can't bring himself to kill an innocent.'

The professor stroked his beard as he walked around Bazalgette's map.

Marshall saw something familiar about the shape that the dots made, it reminded her of a constellation her father had shown her.

'It's Ursa Minor,' she said, drawing an imaginary line between the points on the map with her finger.

'As above, so below!' he exclaimed, clapping his hands. 'Of course!'

Marshall stared at the man, waiting for an explanation.

'The Babylonians called it the "Wagon of Heaven". It's been used by sailors for thousands of years, because of Polaris.'

'The North Star.'

'Exactly!' Gresham moved around the map. 'As above, so below was mentioned in the Emerald Tablet, thought to be one of the oldest alchemical texts. It refers to the influence that the heavens have on the mortal world. Your killer was recreating one of the oldest constellations. Which means he will be holding her somewhere around here.' He picked up a magnifying glass and looked closely at the Isle of Dogs. 'There's a storm water pumping station here at Folly Wall.'

'That's less than half a mile from where they found the van.'

'And it goes into the main sewer.'

84

BELOW

River Thames, London. Monday, December 23. 10:55

Marshall contacted the river police before they left the library. A launch was waiting for them at HMS Wellington Pier.

'We need to get to the Isle of Dogs ASAP,' she said to the skipper as he helped her aboard.

Gresham looked slightly green stepping onto the moving deck.

'You don't like boats?' she asked, sitting down beside him.

'Couldn't we have taken the tube?'

She grinned, there was a devilish glint in her eye. 'This is faster.'

The skipper gunned the engines and they were thrown back into their seats as the boat powered away from the pier.

Moving through the arches of Blackfriars bridge, they passed an open-roofed clipper filled with tourists listening to the gruesome tale of how the body of Roberto Calvi had been found hanging from it in 1982.

Once they were clear of the boat, the captain opened up the throttle and the icy spray took Marshall's breath away. Gresham pulled his coat tighter around him and sheltered down out of the weather, she went forward and stood next to the captain.

'I need to borrow your radio,' she shouted over the sound of the engines.

He handed her the microphone.

'This is DS Marshall, City Police. Can you put me through to DCI Donovan at Wood Street. Over.'

'Received. Patching you through now.'

They hit the bow wave of a passing pleasure cruiser and the boat leaped into the air for a second and she gripped onto the side of the boat.

'Marshall, what the fuck are you doing with the river police?' Donovan's voice came out over the speaker.

'Long story Guv. We're en route to a pumping station on the Isle of Dogs. Near Folly Wall. The professor thinks Fabell's taken Samantha underground.'

'Understood. I'll send backup. Do not attempt to enter the building. Do you hear me?'

'Sorry sir, lost you on that, please repeat?'

She handed the microphone back to the skipper before Donovan could answer and went back to the professor.

Gresham was staring up at Tower Bridge as they swept underneath it.

'I've never seen it from this angle,' he said, the colour slowly returning to his cheeks.

She sat down beside him, tying her hair back with a band.

'We've got less than ten minutes to come up with a plan. What are the chances he's wired the building?'

'I'm not a psychologist, but I'm sure this wasn't part of his Magnus Opus. He'll be thinking on his feet. The pumping station is a safe place, but a temporary one. If he intends to keep her alive he will be thinking about how he can move her.'

The river snaked to the left as they passed Wapping.

'If he's going to move her, it's probably going to be by boat,' Gresham added. 'There's a dock near Harbour Quay. If I were him, I'd be looking to get her on board one of those.' He pointed to a long white cruiser that was making its way towards the skyscrapers of Canary Wharf.

'Or he's going to kill her?'

Gresham shivered, turning the collar of his jacket up against the wind. 'You're the detective. I'm just a historian.'

They beached the boat on the shore opposite The O2. Marshall and Gresham jumped off onto the muddy bank and made their way to the path.

The pumping station was surrounded by a six-foot metal fence. There was no sign of the backup and Marshall wasn't about to wait. She went to the gate and inspected the chain, the links were loose, the padlock looked as if it had been dissolved in acid.

She held it up to Gresham. 'Looks like we're in the right place.'

The gates grated stubbornly as they opened and Marshall slipped between them, pulling them back in place before the professor could follow.

'Stay here and wait for backup.'

He nodded.

. . .

The interior of the building was a vast space, filled with the rhythmic thrum of machinery. Metal gantries loaded with hydro pumping equipment disappeared into the chasm beneath her feet. It reminded her of the Lloyd's building but sunk into the ground.

Looking down, Marshall felt as if she were standing at the top of a tower block. A wave of vertigo swept over her. Gritting her teeth, she made for the staircase and began to descend.

By the third level, the temperature had dropped dramatically. The large pipes around her were freezing to touch and she tried not to imagine what it would be like if the Thames flooded in now. Looking up, she wondered if she could make it back up to the surface in time.

Over the noise of the pumps, she heard the sound of someone crying. It was a woman, and she was close.

Moving quietly amongst the humming machinery, Marshall felt the hairs rising on the back of her neck, as if someone was watching her. She knew that if she waited for the cavalry the situation would escalate and Samantha would end up dead. Her only chance was to try and get to her before they came storming in with their stun grenades and MP5s.

Following the sound of the crying, Marshall came to a small storeroom. The door was locked from the outside, but the bolt slid open easily. Samantha was tied to a camp bed. She was blindfolded and wearing a hospital gown. Marshall realised that Fabell had dressed her like his dead wife.

Coming closer, Marshall could see that her skin was covered in alchemical symbols.

'Samantha, I'm here to help you,' she whispered calmly.

Samantha tried to raise her head from the bed, but her bindings held her down. 'Help me!'

'Shh!' Marshall said, removing the woman's blindfold.

Samantha blinked, staring into her eyes like a new born. Marshall realised that Fabell had removed her makeup and dyed her hair back to its original colour, she hardly looked anything like the woman in the restaurant. 'Who are you?'

'My name is Detective Sergeant Marshall.'

The cable ties were pulled tight around her wrists and legs, cutting into her skin. Marshall looked around for something to cut them with.

The metal shelves in the storeroom were carefully arranged with boxes full of spare parts for various pieces of equipment. There was a set of spanners and some socket sets on the wall, but nothing with a sharp edge.

In the far corner was a desk which Fabell had used to prepare Samantha's meals and medical care. Amongst the cans of half-finished beans and ready meals she found a knife and went back to Sam, who was whimpering.

'He's going to come back soon,' she said. 'When the water comes.'

Marshall had no idea what that meant. 'It's okay,' she assured her, sawing at the plastic ties with the blade.

She managed to free her legs when she heard the rushing sound of water.

'We have to go,' Samantha insisted, looking nervously towards the door. 'He'll be here soon.'

Somewhere above them Marshall heard the whine of the pumps as they kicked in. The sound increased until it was deafening.

Samantha's face went pale, and her mouth widened in a silent scream.

Marshall was too busy working the blade under the tie around Samantha's wrist. It was only as she began to saw that she felt the pin prick in her neck.

'Put the knife down,' she heard him say as a warm sensation spread from the needle and she began to lose the feeling in her hands.

85

CREATION

Folly Wall Pumping Station. Monday, December 23. 12:05

Marshall came around slowly, as if waking from a deep sleep. Her tongue felt strange in her mouth and her head was pounding with the intensity of a tequila-induced hangover.

The rest of her body was numb. Fabell had injected her with some kind of tranquilliser. He was pulling her along a long dark tunnel by the collar of her jacket. As Marshall's eyes adjusted to the dim light, she realised that she was half-immersed in water. The sound of the pumps was nothing more than a distant echo.

'I know you're conscious,' he said, stopping in the middle of the waterway. 'I had to guess your mass. The dose was sufficient to subdue Samantha for thirty minutes and you are virtually the same weight.'

Marshall tried to speak, but her mouth wouldn't co-operate.

His breathing was laboured and she could hear the

strain in his voice. She couldn't move her head and he was staying just out of her eyeline.

'I wanted you all to know what he'd done,' he continued, there was a manic tone in his voice. 'They told me it was an accident. They told me she wasn't in any pain, but there was nothing but pain! For four years she suffered and no one would listen to me.'

He dropped Marshall into the water. She felt the cold flowing over her face and was helpless, unable to move, literally drowning in a foot of water.

Fabell was shouting at her, but she couldn't hear what he was saying.

Marshall closed her eyes and held her breath, unable to push herself up out of the flow.

Time slowed and her lungs began to ache as she tried to ignore the instinct to take a breath.

A hand grabbed the lapels of her jacket and her head broke the surface of the water.

'There had to be a reckoning, do you understand? MacIntyre and Pullman killed her and Sykes covered it up. She deserved justice.'

She opened her eyes. One of his hands went around her neck, lifting her clear of the water and up to his face. It was covered by a ski mask. His blue eyes were fierce and wild, the man was quite clearly insane.

'You were supposed to protect us. But they used their power to change the rules. They believed they were above the law.'

She gasped, filling her lungs with air. He muttered to himself and took hold of her collar once more, dragging her further away from the pumping station.

'I want you to know this. I want you to bear witness to what they have done.'

. . .

Slowly the feeling came back into her fingers. She began to feel the ridges of the pipe beneath her palms as they travelled further into the storm drain. Her sense of smell returned unexpectedly, and she wished it hadn't, the overpowering stench of sewage made her retch.

Fabell brought them to a large junction where many sewers flowed into one. Brown waterfalls cascaded down the walls around her; storm water and effluent from a thousand streets thundered down into a swirling pool below.

Propping her up against a rusting old iron ladder, he fastened her arms to one of the rungs with cable ties.

'We're all pawns in the great game,' he said, pulling off the ski mask and throwing it into the frothing water. 'Abiding by rules set down by men who feel no compunction to follow them.'

He looked so different to Parnell now. In his early fifties, with a sharp, hawkish face and short grey hair. His eyes were haunted, dark circles testifying to the long, sleepless nights he had spent by his wife's bedside.

Taking off his coat and shirt. Marshall saw the marks on his body, he too was covered in symbols. On his chest was the sign of the philosopher's stone.

'I tried so many ways to save her.' Fabell took out a long hunting knife from his jacket. 'But nothing worked. I devoted my life to science and it failed me.'

He came towards her, she couldn't take her eyes off the blade.

'Yet my great work is nearly complete. I have created you, and you will be my truth.' He sliced open the sleeve of her jacket and used the tip of the knife to carve a delicate set of symbols along the inside of her forearm. She could see the blood running down her arm, but felt no pain.

Fabell stepped back, admiring his work. 'Now, you have everything you need to complete this.'

She wanted to ask him what happened, but all she could manage was a mumbled groan.

'Derek Reynolds told me something before he died. He said that all things are connected. He was right. You were always meant to find me and I you. You are the key. Unlock the mystery and give Elizabeth her justice.'

'No!' Marshall managed a strangled cry as he plunged the knife into the centre of the triangle on his chest.

Smiling, he opened his arms wide like a messiah and without another word he fell backward off the ledge and into the torrents below.

86

AFTERMATH

Folly Wall Pumping Station. Monday, December 23. 13:15

It took the team an hour to find her.

Marshall moved in and out of consciousness. When she finally came around she was lying in the back of an ambulance, with medics attending to her wounds.

Donovan was hovering outside, she could hear his voice, he was arguing with Salazar.

'I don't care what you think. Pullman's safe and that's all that matters. Get forensics down here now and stop whingeing. I didn't see you putting yourself in danger to save her.'

Samantha was safe, she thought. *And he's dead*. She shuddered as she remembered the sight of him falling into the water. The heart monitor pinged and the medic looked up from his work.

'Hello,' he said calmly. 'You're okay, I'm just cleaning this up and then I'm going to put a dressing on it.'

She shook her head, forcing a 'No!' from between her dry lips.

The medic looked concerned.

Donovan stepped up into the back of the ambulance. 'Well, if it isn't sleeping beauty.'

'He's dead?'

Donovan nodded. 'Divers found his body trapped against the storm outlet. Nevertheless, I think congratulations are in order.'

'Sir?'

'Samantha Pullman is alive. PDP whisked her off to some private hospital. You I'm afraid have to make do with the NHS's finest.' He slapped the medic on the back.

She lifted her arm, pulling off the dressing. 'Where's Gresham?'

Donovan looked concerned. 'He's outside. Sweet Jesus did he do that to you?'

She nodded. 'Get Gresham.'

Gresham failed to hide the pain when he saw what Fabell had carved into her arm.

There were eight characters, perfectly etched like a skin tattoo into the white flesh of her forearm.

'What does it mean?' Marshall asked.

Gresham stared at the red marks, she watched his eyes flicker back and forth along them.

'Antimony, Arsenic, Bismuth, Magnesium, Phosphorous,' he read aloud, his finger hovering over the red wounds. 'Platinum, Potash — that's Potassium, Zinc.' He looked up at her. 'It's just a list of chemicals.'

'Did Fabell say what this meant?' Donovan asked.

'He mentioned Reynolds. Said that he knew everything.'

'Why Reynolds?'

Marshall shrugged, finding it hard to think clearly, her mind still fogged by the drugs Fabell had given her.

'He said that he created me, as a key, to get justice for his wife.'

'For what? A hit and run?'

Marshall shook her head. 'It was something more. Whatever this is.' She pointed at the symbols. 'It's supposed to lead me to the truth.'

Donovan frowned. 'The only place you're going is to the hospital.'

She sat up too quickly, her head spinning. 'Someone else is in danger. I don't think he's finished.'

'I think it might be a code,' Gresham interrupted, showing them his phone. There was a grid of letters laid out across the screen. 'Using the equivalent periodic table symbol for each element it spells out. 'SbAsBiMgPPtKZn.'

Donovan scowled. 'Just a bunch of gobbledegook.'

'Or it might be a password?' Marshall wondered, 'for Reynolds's hard drive.'

87

UNLOCKED

Wood Street Station, London. Monday, December 23. 15:45

Frazer smiled as they entered his lab. He looked as though a huge weight had been lifted off his shoulders.

'You look like shit!'

Marshall smiled. 'Thanks, I probably smell like it too. Did it work?'

Frazer shook his head. 'Not the first time, but you were on the right track. I substituted some of the elements for their atomic weights. It took less than an hour to work out the right combination.'

Proudly, he turned back to his desk, the code: **'Sb 22 Bi 12 P 78 K Zn'** was displayed on one screen.

On a separate monitor was a directory of folders, each labelled with one of the victim's names.

'Reynolds knew them all,' Frazer said, double-clicking on Melanie Gladwell's.

It opened to show a grid of various documents and

photographs. There were messages between Melanie and her lover, bank statements and even her husband's medical records.

Marshall pointed to a folder name after Sykes. 'Open that one.'

The folder was filled with police reports and CCTV videos. Frazer clicked on one. It showed a street late at night, the timecode on it read 23:02, Elizabeth Fabell was walking along St Mary Axe, directly past the church.

Marshall recognised Melanie standing on the other side of the road, looking as if she was waiting for a taxi. As Elizabeth stepped off the curb a car came careering around the corner and struck her, sending her spinning over its bonnet and onto the road.

The car didn't stop and they could see Melanie running over to Elizabeth and kneeling down beside the limp body.

'She witnessed the accident,' Marshall said to Biggs. 'That's why he cut out her tongue. Frazer, can you go back and see if you can get a clear shot of the number plate?'

Frazer slowly rewound the video until he had the front of the car in a clear shot. There were two people in the silver Mercedes, although they couldn't see their faces, Marshall could tell it was a man driving.

Biggs checked his notes. 'The registration matches MacIntyre's car, the one that was totalled an hour later.'

'So he made his wife take the blame for it. No wonder she divorced him.'

'But why did Sykes cover it up?' Biggs asked.

Marshall scoffed. 'Because Lord Pullman paid him a shit ton of money.'

'Why Pullman?'

Marshall tapped on the pixellated screen. 'I'm betting that's not Mrs MacIntyre in the passenger seat.'

'You think he was shagging Samantha?'

Marshall shrugged. 'I think he was coked off his tits when he hit Fabell.'

'And she called Daddy?'

While they were talking, Frazer had been scanning through another folder. 'There's a ton of stuff on Pullman.'

'Samantha?' Marshall asked, turning back to the screen. There were hundreds of documents, bank statements and scans of international transactions and shipping notes.

'These are her father's companies. Did Reynolds hack into his private email?'

Frazer shook his head. 'Those files belong to Elizabeth Fabell.' He pulled up a list of emails to her boss, all were dated over five years ago.

Marshall read one of the emails. It questioned a series of transactions between gold dealers in Belgium and a company in Qatar. From her tone, it was clear that Elizabeth Fabell was concerned about the deals — apparently they had all the hallmarks of money laundering.

'So maybe it wasn't an accident? Maybe MacIntyre was trying to kill her.'

'Why would he get involved?' Frazer asked.

'Because Lord Pullman was one of his biggest clients?' Biggs suggested.

88

CASE CLOSED

Wood Street Station, London. Tuesday, December 24. 09:00

Donovan stared at the whiteboard while Marshall reorganised the images of the victims, placing Elizabeth Fabell in the centre.

'You think Reynolds was blackmailing them?' he asked.

'Possibly, he certainly hacked into their accounts while he was working at Lloyd's five years ago. He saw everything.'

'So Fabell took his eyes?'

Marshall nodded. 'And Melanie's tongue, because she never told the truth.'

'What about Sykes? Why did he try and dissolve him?'

'Because he was the one that made it all disappear.'

Donovan raised his eyebrows. 'Still doesn't explain why he killed MacIntyre's wife.'

'I think she must have gone to see him after his wife died. Someone had to have told Fabell about the conspiracy. Perhaps it was her way of getting some payback on her ex-husband and the Pullmans. Gates found traces of her blood in Fabell's chest freezer.'

'And you think MacIntyre intentionally tried to murder Elizabeth Fabell because of what she had discovered about Pullman's trading?'

'Lord Pullman was one of MacIntyre's biggest clients, and he was shagging his daughter, it's too much of a coincidence.'

Donovan rubbed his hands together. 'Sounds like you've got it all covered. Think we can close the case?'

'We've passed Elizabeth's findings on to NCA. They're going to follow up on the deals that she uncovered, but there is one last thing that's bothering me.'

'About?'

'There's one victim missing. He marked them with air, water and fire but not earth.'

Donovan frowned. 'Go home Marshall. Try and get a break over Christmas, you deserve it.'

Bah humbug.

89

GOODBYES

Wales. New Year's Day.

Her father's funeral was a small family affair at a church near where he was born in Porthcawl, Wales.

It was a bleak day, the sky was a slate grey, threatening rain but never delivering.

They walked behind the hearse up the hill to the chapel. Her mother holding on to her as if she were about to collapse. Marshall had never seen her quite so fragile, not in all the years since he'd got ill. There was always a glimmer of hope in her eyes, that somehow he was going to get better.

Will's family had come too. She hadn't seen them since the day of his funeral over seventeen years ago. His mother looked worn, as if time and the grieving for her son had prematurely aged her. She smiled weakly as they passed at the chapel door. His dad ignored her, she could still see the anger burning behind his hard granite eyes. They had nothing but their pain to keep them going — it had become their life.

James was sitting on one of the pews at the back.

Marshall saw her mother to her seat near the front, next to her sister and went back to him.

'Thanks for coming,' she said, sitting down beside him.

'Sorry,' he said, taking her hand. 'He was a great bloke.'

The touch of his warm hand on hers felt good. She wanted to put her arms around him, but she stopped herself. There was a barrier between them now, a tiny but unbreakable distance.

'He was. I think he would have made a great grandad.'

James nodded and squeezed her hand. 'Did you tell them?'

'No, it would have broken their hearts. All they ever wanted was a grandchild.'

'We could try again.'

She shook her head, hiding the tears that were welling up in her eyes. 'No. We can't.'

Marshall let go of his hand and stood up. 'I need to get back to Mum. Will you stay for the wake?'

He nodded.

She read the eulogy, and the priest ended with the Lord's prayer. Her father had never been a religious person, but there was something about the tradition that comforted her mother.

As he spoke the line: 'On earth, as it is in heaven.' Marshall realised how close it was to something that Gresham had said. 'As above, so below.'

90

INSPECTOR

Marshall rented a small cottage on the Gower Peninsula, near where her father had grown up and spent some time with her mum putting his estate in order. Bills and bank accounts, credit cards and tax. All the stuff that most people take for granted, it all had to be sorted out. Everyone had to be told of his passing.

She took some comfort from the banality of the forms and the endless phone calls. Her mother sat at the window and watched the sea. They went for long walks and talked about him and cried, not hysterically, but still deeply, letting the grief slowly drain until it was more like a soft ache.

Three weeks later, Marshall returned to work.

The incident room had been cleared down, all the files boxed up and sent to the archives.

Biggs was at his desk looking through a report when she walked in. He smiled and held up a large cup of coffee with her name on it.

'Thanks. How's it been?' she asked, taking the drink.

His eyes widened. 'You haven't heard?'

'No. Been off the grid.'

Biggs leaned in close. 'Salazar's gone. Donovan had her transferred. She's gone to Thames Valley.'

Marshall looked over at the DCI's office.

'Who's he bringing in?'

Biggs stared at her, his eyes gleaming. 'Who do you think?'

'Marshall, can I see you for a moment please?' Donovan was standing at his door, beckoning her to come in.

'Good luck, Inspector,' Biggs said with a wink.

91

WHISKEY

Houses of Parliament, London. Thursday, January 23. 16:00

Lord Pullman sat in his office sipping a large whisky and watching the gold market trades on his screen.

'Detective Marshall is here sir. She wishes to speak with you,' his receptionist's voice chimed through the intercom.

'Does she have a warrant?'

'She does.'

He put the drink down, closed the trading application and locked his PC.

'Send her in and contact the lawyers.'

Marshall had two other officers with her when she entered the room. This was an official visit and she wanted him to know it.

'Detective Sergeant Marshall,' Pullman acknowledged. 'To what do I owe the pleasure?'

'Detective Inspector,' Marshall corrected him with a polite smile. 'Lord Pullman, we have a number of questions relating to an attempted murder of Elizabeth Fabell in 2014.'

He raised an eyebrow, this was obviously not what he was expecting.

'Please take a seat.'

'I'd prefer to stand.'

Pullman shrugged nonchalantly and sat behind his desk. 'I'm sorry but I don't know anyone by the name of Fabell.'

Marshall produced a set of print outs and laid them on the desk.

'She was an accountant at KPMG. She found discrepancies with certain transactions made by some of your companies.'

His eyes scanned over the documents, but he resisted the urge to pick them up.

'Surely this is a matter for the finance department?'

Marshall produced another photograph. It was an enhanced image of MacIntyre and a woman driving a silver Bentley. 'This is from CCTV footage that was erased by DI Sykes. It clearly shows William MacIntyre and a woman driving away from the scene of the accident in which Elizabeth was knocked down.'

'MacIntyre is dead,' Pullman said curtly. 'What has this got to do with me?'

'There was a witness at the scene, Melanie Gladwell, one of your companies paid her over a million pounds shortly after that incident.' She placed a bank transfer onto the desk. 'Separate payments were also made to DI Sykes and eventually to an IT consultant by the name of Reynolds. Who I believe was blackmailing you.'

'Again. This is all circumstantial.'

'Reynolds hacked into the accounts of everyone who was involved. Including your phone.'

She produced a final document, a transcript of a series of text messages from Samantha.

'Daddy. Mac killed her,' Marshall read aloud. 'Please help.'

Pullman sighed and rubbed his eyes.

92

EARTH

Marshall looked down at the grave stone. The wording chiselled into the dark grey marble read:

Elizabeth Mary Fabell, 1980 - 2019.
As above, so below.

Below the words was a small downward pointing triangle with a horizontal line through the lower point.

'So she was the first victim?'

'Earth,' Gresham said, taking her hand.

'He saved Samantha's baby.' Her other hand stroking her stomach instinctively.

'The renewal of life is sacred to an alchemist.'

'More likely it reminded him of his own wife.'

They walked back through the woods to his car. It was still snowing, covering the cemetery with a blanket of white.

Opening the door of the old E-Type Jaguar, he paused. 'I was wondering if you would like to join me for dinner? I have an annual fellows' dinner at Christ Church. It's terribly old fashioned, but the food is magnificent and the wine cellar can be traced back to the sixteenth century.'

'Do I have to wear a dress?'

He smiled. 'Most of the other dons will be.'

Marshall laughed, it was the first time in she couldn't remember how long.

'Sure, why not?'

Detective Marshall returns in The Weighing of the Heart

ALSO BY KAREN HASTIE

As Above, So Below

The Weighing of the Heart

Human Trials

ACKNOWLEDGMENTS

Thanks to everyone who has helped to make this book come to life. To my family for their advice, and friends for all their comments!

I hope you enjoyed it. Please don't forget to leave a review!

Thanks,
Karen x

Printed in Great Britain
by Amazon

59801140R00189